Moments later, she felt heightened awareness.

She knew before Cole stood beside her.

"What games are you playing?" he asked.

"So now you know me?" she asked before taking a sip of her champagne.

"I never knew you to play games, Jillian, but then I realized too late I never knew you at all," he said, his voice low enough for just her ears and cold enough to chill her to her bones.

Sadness waved over her, but she stiffened her spine and turned sideways to face his profile.

Cole turned his head to look at her.

Their eyes met. She shivered.

"Jillian?"

The sound of her name on his lips again was her undoing. Missing him? Desiring him? Wanting to sex him?

Fine.

Falling in love?

That was not a part of the plan.

Dear Reader,

I'm happy to present another "Sexy, Funny & Oh So Real" romance novel to you. After more than twenty years of writing about love, I am just as invested in romance as I was when I wrote my first book so long ago. Thank you to those of you who have been on this ride with me from the beginning and many welcomes to those just discovering my brand of romance for the first time.

The Rebel Heir continues the scandalous story of the Cress family but also warms you with yet another story of love. This time it's the rebel son, Cole, and the family's ambitious personal chef, Jillian. A yearlong no-strings steamy dalliance is shattered when Jillian chooses advancing her career over Cole—but she also discovers with the distance now between them that it was her heart that Cole had claimed and not just her body. Now she must fight to prove to him that love can—and *will*—conquer all.

Sit back in a quiet spot, tuck your feet beneath your bottom and sip from the drink of your choice as you escape into this story delivering plenty of chemistry, a good chuckle or two, the scandal and secrets of the rich, and some of the steamiest love scenes you will ever encounter. Hopefully you'll thank me later for a romance story that will captivate you from the first page to the very last.

What's better than happily-ever-after?

Best,

N.

NIOBIA BRYANT

THE REBEL HEIR

HARLEQUIN
DESIRE

ISBN-13: 978-1-335-23292-2

The Rebel Heir

For questions and comments about the quality of this book, please contact us at CustomerService@Harlequin.com.

Harlequin Enterprises ULC
22 Adelaide St. West, 40th Floor
Toronto, Ontario M5H 4E3, Canada
www.Harlequin.com

Printed in U.S.A.

Recycling programs for this product may not exist in your area.

Niobia Bryant is the award-winning and nationally bestselling author of more than forty-five works of romance and commercial mainstream fiction. Twice she has won the RT Reviewers' Choice Best Book Award for African American/Multicultural Romance. Her books have appeared in *Ebony*, *Essence*, *New York Post*, *The Star-Ledger*, *Dallas Morning News* and many other national publications. One of her bestselling books was adapted to film.

Books by Niobia Bryant

Harlequin Desire

One Night with Cinderella
The Rebel Heir

Harlequin Kimani

A Billionaire Affair
Tempting the Billionaire

Visit the Author Profile page at Harlequin.com, or niobiabryant.com, for more titles.

You can also find Niobia Bryant on Facebook, along with other Harlequin Desire authors, at Facebook.com/harlequindesireauthors!

This one is dedicated to the
wonderful thing called love.

One

Jillian Rossi pushed her tortoiseshell spectacles up on her nose as she looked over the rim of her cup of coffee at the spacious chef's kitchen of the townhouse in the prominent, historic Lenox Hill section of Manhattan's Upper East Side. She eyed the dark wood custom cabinets against the light walls, chrome appliances and bronzed fixtures. She loved the space. Knew it well from working as the private chef to its owners for the last year.

Not that she wasn't used to working for the wealthy and famous.

After many years of learning about cooking at the elbow of Ionie, her beloved grandmother, Jillian had gone on to culinary school with a dream of one day opening her own restaurant. Social media success garnered for posting home-cooked savory meals and delicious desserts led to her traveling the world as a personal chef for well-known athletes and celebrities— waylaying her restaurant dreams. Yacht parties. Elaborate dinners. Whirlwind events during award season. Private jets. Mansions. Penthouse apartments. Private islands. Celebrities.

"Lifestyle of the rich and famous," Jillian sighed.

Several years later she'd left being a part of the more glamorous side of life to finally open her restaurant, assuming her days serving as a private chef were over. Unfortunately, the venture had bombed, leaving her in massive debt just a year after its opening. The sting of disappointment and embarrassment from her failure was all too familiar, and the past year had not lessened it any—nor had the return to work as a private chef.

She loved cooking. And, considering the Cress family were world-renowned chefs, they seemed to enjoy the meals she prepared without question. Jillian took that as a feather in her cap. She just considered the position a step backward in her career path.

Been there. Done that. Now I'm doing it again.

Jillian crossed the kitchen to enter the large pantry to the right. Here there were custom cabinets filled with perfectly organized essentials. The counters were marble-topped and beneath one section there was an under-the-counter commercial-size freezer. There was also a large rinse sink to handle food prep if necessary.

As she moved to the office area set up for her, she

checked the laser printer to ensure the cream heavy-bond paper with its gold, raised monogram was loaded. Using the touch screen computer, Jillian printed off copies of the breakfast menu. One for each family member's platinum-rimmed place setting.

She was used to the grand nature of it all.

Being in such luxurious surroundings by such an accomplished Cress family only furthered her desire to succeed. The former chefs now operated a multimillion-dollar culinary empire. They also owned this five-story, ten-thousand-square-foot townhouse, which was large enough to accommodate the entire brood. The parents, Phillip Senior and Nicolette. The five sons: Phillip Junior and his wife, Raquel, and their four-year-old daughter Collette, Sean, Gabriel, Lucas and—

"Morning, Jillian."

Cole.

At the deep sound of the voice of Coleman Cress, she paused for one telling second before reaching to remove the printed menus. The pace of her heart sped up as she looked over her shoulder to see him standing in the open doorway. Filling it with ease.

Like his four brothers, Cole was a handsome man with a tall, lean, toned warrior-like physique. He had almond-shaped eyes of a grayish-blue against his medium-brown complexion. His good looks were best described as *chiseled*—from his high cheekbones and broad nose to his square jawline. But there was a complementary softness to his full mouth and the long lashes framing those eyes. He kept his dark brown curly hair cut low, the shadow of a beard and mustache intensifying his magnetism. His clothing preference—normally dark T-shirts, denims and leather motorcycle jackets—gave him just the right amount of edge to draw long glances.

Often, Jillian found his looks similar to that of the actor Michael Ealy.

Just pure goodness.

Her pulse raced. "Good morning, Mr. Cress," she said as he stepped inside the pantry and closed the door behind him. She extended her arm to hand him a menu. "Omelets for breakfast. Here's the list of the choices of ingredients."

Cole locked eyes with her and smiled, as smooth as syrup spreading across warm pancakes. A knowing smile. A charming one with just a hint of the wile of a wolf. "Mr. Cress?" he mocked as he strolled across the pantry to stand before her, ignoring the paper. "Why so formal? Last night it was Cole."

Cole, don't stop. Don't you dare stop.

She forced herself to break their gaze, shivering in her awareness of him, and flushed with heat at the memory. Over the last year they had shared many. Hotly. Secretly.

Cole eased his large hands beneath her monogrammed chef's coat and settled them on her hips. She felt the heat of his touch through the black leggings she wore. "Tell me you don't want to kiss me," he whispered against her mouth as he lowered his head.

She closed her eyes and waited to feel his mouth with sweet anticipation.

His kisses are the absolute best.

"We can't," she whispered, stepping back before that glorious mouth of his could land.

Cole paused before taking a step that would close the gap she'd put between them. "I hate that you're right," he admitted, letting his eyes linger with apparent regret on her mouth before turning and exiting the pantry, leaving the door ajar.

Jillian released a little breath and bit her bottom lip as she watched him walk away in his bow-legged swagger. She waited for her pulse to cease racing. Cole had that effect on her. With him near her or just in her line of vision, she lost control.

He had been hard to deny since the first time she'd laid eyes on him. Last January. When she'd been hired. For the next two months, they'd shared long looks that had hinted at their mutual interest. By March, they'd been in a deep, no-holds-barred, no-strings-attached fling. A year later, as a woman in touch with her sexuality and not looking for anything serious after two failed marriages in her youth, she was still enjoying her hot, passionate, secret affair with the rebel Cress son.

Still, anything serious with him was not a part of her plan.

Clearing her throat, Jillian collected the printed menus and carried the stack out of the pantry. She walked to the dining room at the rear of the house with its elaborate glass wall as Nicolette Lavoie-Cress stepped off the elevator in the corner to her right beside the staircase. "Good morning, Mrs. Cress," she said, giving a polite nod to the middle-aged, olive-skinned French beauty with silver-streaked blond hair and bluish eyes like Cole's. "I was just putting out the breakfast menus."

Nicolette nodded. "Very good," she said with her heavy French accent. "For dinner, I am expecting the entire family...except Gabe."

Jillian was well aware that Gabriel Cress had moved out of the family home after a massive fall out with Phillip Senior. He had not been back to the townhouse, not even for the fall and winter holidays. Cole had also revealed that Gabe was still with Monica, the Cress family's former housekeeper for the past five years.

But she made sure her face revealed none of that awareness or that the woman's regret was clear.

"The temperature is finally starting to warm up, so let's do some kind of pasta," Nicolette said.

Phillip Senior, a tall, solid, dark-skinned man with broad features and a bright smile, stepped into the kitchen. He was from England and had met Nicolette when they both attended culinary school in Paris. He shared an intimate look with his wife before he gave Jillian a formal nod of greeting and continued into the dining room. He claimed his seat at the head of the long table for ten, topped with charcoal leather and surrounded by steel-blue-suede armless chairs.

"How about seafood linguine with squid, mussels, clams, shrimp, scallops and lobster?" Jillian offered, wanting to reclaim the woman's attention.

Jillian found her to be sophisticated and composed unless communicating with her husband. Her love for Phillip Cress Senior was of no question, nor his for her. Neither tried to hide their affection for one another.

"Merveilleux," Nicolette said, moving across the kitchen to the dining room, as well.

Jillian, pleased that she thought it *wonderful*, followed behind and quickly moved around the table to set a menu on each place setting. Cole, swiping through his phone, did not look up when she put one before him. She held no curiosity about what had his attention. She neither wanted nor claimed ownership to a wild, rebellious man like Coleman Cress.

That would be ludicrous.

Jillian no longer trusted her love goggles. In truth, she'd shattered them under her foot, determined not to have yet another failed relationship thanks to childhood fantasies of a romance like that of her parents, who'd been together since high school. For now, Cole Cress and his eight-pack abs were all about fun distraction and nothing more.

And what could be more fun than lovemaking made all the more daring with whipped cream, taking long motorcycle rides through Manhattan, or bathing together in hot, scented water filled with flower petals.

As the rest of the family entered the dining room, Jillian cleared her thoughts and headed to the kitchen.

"Good morning, Chef Jillian!"

She smiled down at the happy face of Collette with her dimpled cheeks, bright yellow spectacles and big toothy smile. Phillip Junior and Raquel's four-year-old daughter was completely adorable.

"No-no," Nicolette gently reprimanded her granddaughter from her seat at the end of the table opposite her husband.

"Oops," Collette said, giggling as she briefly pressed her hands to her mouth. "*Bonjour*, Chef Jillian."

Nicolette, Jillian knew, was teaching French to the little one.

"*Bonjour*, Collette," she returned warmly before continuing into the kitchen to retrieve a crystal carafe of her fresh-squeezed citrus juice and a warming carafe of Ghanaian coffee.

She eyed Felice, the live-in housekeeper who'd replaced Monica, in the den attached to the kitchen's east side in the spacious open floor plan. Like Jillian, the older woman focused on her daily duties. She wasn't as pleasant as Monica, but she got her work done, which was all that mattered.

"I see that you insist on dressing like a derelict, Coleman," Phillip Senior said in his British accent.

Jillian paused because the annoyance in the patriarch's voice was unmistakable. All of the other sons wore suits and held a more professional demeanor. Cole's insistence on not doing so was a constant thorn in his father's side.

Cole shifted his eyes up from his phone to glare down the table at his father. "If you mean comfortable and of my choosing as a grown man, then yes," he said, his tone cold.

It was like watching day transform into night in an instant. Cole was charming and friendly, a charismatic gentleman—except in his interactions with his father. He seemed to enjoy antagonizing him.

"Life is all about the choices we make," Cole continued.

Phillip Senior's eyes narrowed to slits and the movement of his cheeks evidenced his clenched teeth.

Nicolette looked over and saw Jillian standing there.

"Phillip, I'm sure this can wait," Nicolette said.

Translation: not in front of the staff.

At the woman's movement of her fingers to enter, Jillian walked into the room as Cole broke his hard stare with Phillip Senior to return his attention to his phone. The wealthy playboy was always quick with a joke or sardonic comment and seemed to relish being the rebel in his family. She doubted he took anything seriously.

And thus why, for her, their connection was all about really great, super-spontaneous, hot sex. Cole was beautiful with his muscled body and sexy as all get-out. And he knew how to please her—in fact, he seemed to thrive on it.

Damn.

Jillian fought the urge to shiver in desire. That was the Cole effect. Just the very thought of his lovemaking was enough to awaken her privates. "Okay…" she began with a lick of her lips. "We have a nice selection of ingredients for omelets along with Lyonnaise potatoes. Also, there are fresh seasonal fruit cups in a light honey and your choice of toast."

"Just egg white with spinach and a little mozzarella for me," Lucas said before reaching for the citrus juice to pour himself a small glass.

That wasn't surprising. The youngest Cress brother had shed fifty pounds and seemed dedicated to keeping the weight off—and his string of pliable women on.

As she took everyone's choice, Jillian's eyes kept going

to Cole. She could tell from the stiffness of his shoulders that he was annoyed. He'd always spoken highly of her pan-fried potatoes sautéed with caramelized onions and butter. She served them for breakfast or dinner, along with a steak.

He won't be ready to eat, though.

"Cole, what type of omelet would you like?" she asked.

He looked up at her. His shoulders softened and he smiled. A new switch from night to day. "I'll pass on breakfast. Just coffee is fine," he said with a seemingly polite smile.

Jillian's knowledge that she was right about his eating habit being affected by his mood surprised her. With a nod, she turned and walked back across the vast space to the eight-burner Viking stove to heat and oil eight omelet pans straight from the Cress, INC. line of cookware. Quickly she cracked two eggs into each of eight ceramic bowls, added salt and black pepper with heavy cream before whisking each swiftly then pouring them into the pans.

Leaving the eggs to set and cook on low-medium heat, she opened her leather case to reveal her engraved all-metal knife set…and a note card monogrammed with the Cress, INC. logo. She held the card to her nose and inhaled the subtle scent of Cole's cologne still clinging to it. Like her sheets after he spent a night at her apartment.

She opened the card and mouthed the words as she read them to herself. "Last night before I left you, I kept the panties you were wearing. I want to enjoy the smell of you."

The thrill she felt was addictive.

She looked over into the dining room and caught his eyes on her. He patted the pocket of the leather jacket he wore before raising his cup of coffee in a toast. She flushed with warmth. But, forcing herself to focus on flipping the omelets and adding the ingredients atop one side of each, she was unable to slow the pounding of her heart at the thought of Cole in possession of her sheer red panties.

Over the rim of his cup, Cole surreptitiously eyed Jillian as she left the dining room. She was a tall and slender bronzed beauty with her auburn curly hair pulled up into a topknot. The glasses she wore while cooking couldn't hide the long, thick lashes that framed her round brown eyes. Her cheekbones were high, and her chin narrow, giving her face a heart shape that lent emphasis to her full pouty, perfectly kissable mouth. The back and forth movement of her buttocks in her black leggings enticed him. He smiled into the cup. It was an even more glorious sight free of clothing and gripped in his hands.

Damn.

Jillian was beautiful and curvy. Funny and feisty. Sexy. Insatiable. And not searching for her happily-ever-after.

Perfect.

He thoroughly enjoyed flirting with her before they found hot moments to relieve the sexual tension that pulsed between them. But he was not looking for love.

Been there. Done that.

When he'd met Traci Mason during his senior year at culinary school, Cole had believed he'd found a stunning, intelligent, loyal beauty with whom he could plan a future. He'd even purchased a ring and planned a huge engagement surprise via hot-air balloon. Then his brother, Gabriel let him know Traci was quite vocal with her friends that she had landed a big fish from the wealthy Cress family and planned to ride the wave to her own successful career.

Any doubts Cole had had about the veracity of the gossip were erased when Gabriel played him a video, taken without Traci's knowledge, of her saying just that. And more. Much more.

It was clear that she'd seen Cole as a pathway to success and not as a man to truly love.

That had been his last serious relationship and he'd preferred no strings attached ever since. His sexy, secretive dalliances with the family's beautiful chef for the past year had been his escape as his family had become unrecognizable. His father's announcement that he was stepping down as the chief executive officer of Cress, INC., and would name one of his five sons as his successor, had put the brothers at odds with one another. Gone was the notion of loyalty. Each was in search of Phillip Cress Senior's deeming him meritorious of the throne.

Cole couldn't deny that it was a worthy empire.

His parents had devoted more than fifty years to build a reputation as celebrated and well-respected chefs, won Michelin stars and James Beard awards, established many successful restaurants, and written more than two dozen bestselling cookbooks and culinary guides. In a calculated move that had paid off, they'd shifted their focus to establishing Cress, INC. And, within just a few years, had successfully diversified into production of their own nationally syndicated cooking shows, cookware, online magazines, an accredited cooking school and a nonprofit foundation.

Like their parents, the five Cress brothers had become chefs—all acclaimed, as well. Four years ago, upon their parents' earnest request, each son had left behind his career to claim a full-time role as a member of the business's executive team. The eldest brother, Phillip Junior, ran the nonprofit, the Cress Family Foundation. Gabriel had stepped down from overseeing the restaurant division to fulfill his dreams of owning and operating his own eatery. Sean supervised the syndicated cooking shows. The youngest, Lucas, was head of the cookware line.

And Cole served as president of Cress, INC.'s digital marketing and global branding, overseeing a small team that managed publicity and marketing as well as the company's websites and online presence. He'd taken the position at his mother's urging to participate in something along with his beloved brothers.

In time, he had come to enjoy the work and taken pride in the company's exponential growth in online traffic and analytics. In truth, he cared nothing about the CEO position and had only competed for it because he felt his father didn't believe he could do it. Unlike his brothers, his desire to create and cook was too strong to ignore. Thus, his food truck purchase and operation on the weekends—another bane to his father, who found the very idea of the food truck industry beneath chefs of Cress caliber.

An outdated and judgmental notion.

And he's the last man to hold everyone else to such damn high standards.

Cole set his cup down on the saucer as he spared his father a glance just as the man looked down the length of the table to give his wife a warm smile. The anger he felt with his father—the same ire that had spurned his rebellious nature since his teenage years—burned like fire in his gut.

Liar.

Phillip Senior was a formidable man who was very aware that he was raising men. He loved his boys, but the only softness and warmth he showed in abundance was to their mother. There had been little tolerance for whining, misbehaving, mistruths or weakness from his sons.

Cole looked to one of the two empty chairs at the table. The normal seat of his older brother, Gabe, was empty. He was proud of him for standing up to the disparaging way his father had spoken of Monica upon discovering his son had dared to date the help.

Cole felt his stomach burn at the memory...

"Is she the reason for your insanity lately?" Phillip roared, the veins of his neck seemingly strained.

"She's the reason I'm happy," Gabe returned calmly.

"Happy or horny?"

"Both."

Cole chuckled, which incensed his father even more, yet his other brothers sat as if afraid to speak up. Their silence angered Cole. Gone was their alliance as brothers.

"There are women you wed and those you bed. Know the difference. And that goes for all of you," Phillip said.

Gabe angrily strode over to his father, standing toe-to-toe to confront him. "Don't disrespect her in that way." His voice was cold. "I tolerate a lot from you, but I will not put up with that."

Knowing Gabe was "The Good One," offering no trouble and never a cross word to his parents, it had been exhilarating to watch him challenge their father. In the same manner, Cole wished he had been brave enough to do the same in the past.

As his family members' conversation continued around the table, Cole, lost in his thoughts, took another deep sip of the brew. He barely noticed his grip on the rim of his cup had tightened. Once he did, he released it. The cup dropped down onto the saucer. He had to catch it before it tipped and spilled its hot contents.

Every eye was on him.

"Quelque chose ne va pas, Oncle Cole?"

At his niece's question, Cole looked down at her, looking up at him through her bright spectacles from her usual seat beside him at the table. He smiled at her with warmth. "Nothing's wrong, Collie," he assured her.

"You seemed moodier than usual," Nicolette observed, giving him an encouraging smile. "I know you love Jillian's potatoes. Not feeling well?"

"Don't spoil him, Nicolette."

Cole tensed at his father's terse reprimand. "Spoiled is believing you can have anything you want, when and where you want it," he snapped, sitting back against his chair.

Phillip Senior glared at him before shaking his head and returning his attention to the print newspapers he still favored.

Cole didn't miss his brothers Lucas and Sean share a look. Phillip Junior frowned and his wife pretended not to notice. Collette was lost to the tension.

The father-son contentious relationship was nothing new. In truth, the root of Cole's problem with his father was more than a rebellion. It was a bitter disappointment.

As a teenager, Cole had visited the family's restaurant and walked in on his father cheating on his mother with one of the waitresses. Visions of their half-clothed bodies rutting away flashed in his mind's eye and he winced at the memory and forced it out.

He'd never shared the secret of his father's affair. At times, he hated himself for that.

Cole looked at his mother. A devoted beauty whose feelings for her husband were clear. Her love. And her loyalty.

He hadn't wanted to hurt her, but his anger at his father for betraying her had been stewing for years.

Cole had been determined to be a better man to Traci before he'd discovered she was using him. Although he knew his reputation in the press was now that of a playboy, Cole never juggled more than one woman at a time—he just kept his relationships strings-free.

"Can I get anything for anyone before I go shopping for dinner?"

Cole glanced up at Jillian, standing in the opening of the dining room, before he looked over his shoulder at the spring sun blazing down on the thirty-two-foot length of the garden. A long concrete table set beneath an arched framework covered with bamboo leaves offered privacy and shade. At night, he liked to sit outside, smoke a cigar and sip Uncle Nearest premium whiskey as he listened to the sounds of New York and watched the illuminated water fountain at the end of the garden.

There had been many a night that memories of stolen moments with the sexy chef had dominated his thoughts. More often than not, that led to a phone call or text before he was off on his motorcycle, zipping through the streets to reach her.

And stroke deeply inside her...

"That will be all, Jillian. Thank you," Nicolette said, breaking into his train of thought.

"We need someone to step in and take over the restaurant division in Gabe's absence," Phillip Senior said, wiping the corners of his mouth with his napkin before dropping it atop his half-eaten steak, mushroom and mozzarella omelet.

Cole glared at his father. "Good luck with that," he drawled. "I'm not filling a spot my brother left."

"Grow up, Cole!" Phillip Junior snapped.

Cole shot him a glare, as well. "Go to—"

"Oh no-oo," Raquel said, rising in a beautiful sheer

red shirt and matching wide-legs pants to pick up their daughter's plate. "Come on, Collette. We'll finish breakfast upstairs."

"What's wrong?" the little girl asked.

"The adults need the room…and to remember *they* are adults." Raquel shot a meaningful glance at both Cole and her husband before leading the preschooler out of the room.

"This sullen brat routine is getting old, Cole," Phillip Junior said, looking even more like the former wrestler turned movie star Dwayne "The Rock" Johnson. He hated it when his brothers teased him about that.

"And so is figuring out just how you manage to breathe with your face buried so deep in Dad's behind," Cole shot back.

Of all the brothers, Phillip Junior was the most devoted to his father—and believed that being "The Eldest" guaranteed him a natural progression to the throne.

"Enough," Sean said sternly with a shake of his head.

Cole eyed "The Star." Everyone had a role. Sean relished his as the star of several of Cress, INC's most popular cooking shows. He believed his face as the brand was the winning ticket. "Enough what?" he asked.

"Enough making everything uncomfortable because it amuses you," Lucas answered.

I find humor to avoid rage. But Cole kept his thought to himself as he eyed the youngest Cress son, "The Favorite." All his life, Lucas had been doted on by their mother with love—and plenty of food. He'd packed the extra pounds on until recently.

Cole loved his brothers. His only anger with them was for their blind allegiance to their father, who was undeserving of it.

No one knows that but me.

"So, you all will just fill Gabe's shoes and make him feel we don't want or need him back?" Cole accused, eyeing each of his brothers.

"À la nourriture. À la vie. À l'amour," Nicolette said, filling the silence with her favorite French saying. To food. To life. To love.

The maxim was painted on the wall above all of her stoves—personal and professional—and on the base of every pan in the Cress line of cookware. It was the watermark of every letter from the various editors of their culinary magazines. It was also branded throughout their online presence. And it served as the closing statement for the cooking shows produced by Cress, INC.'s television division.

"Gabriel will return," she asserted. "His presence here and at Cress, INC. is missed. Until he decides that he wants his position back, someone must complete the work."

"I'll do it," Phillip Junior asserted. "A future CEO has to set the example and step in when left in a jam by someone else."

"Sycophant," Cole muttered, disgusted by the lack of loyalty among brothers.

Nicolette reached to cover Cole's hand with her own. "I miss him, too," she assured him.

"Then fix it," he demanded, locking his gray-blue eyes with her own.

Her gaze softened as she nodded. "I think you're right," she admitted.

"Nicolette!" Phillip Senior roared.

"Assez, c'est assez, mon amour," she said, looking down the length of the table at her husband.

Like their parents, the brothers spoke both French and Spanish fluently.

Enough is enough, my love.

And though her tone was soft, there was no denying the finality of her words.

Two

One month later

"Enjoying your meal?"

Jillian looked up at the striking figure of Lorenzo León Cortez, Gabriel's best friend. His voice was deep, and he was tall—well over six feet—with broad shoulders and bone-straight, waist-length hair that only accentuated handsome features of his Native American and Mexican heritage.

The man was truly magnificent.

"It was delicious," she admitted, smiling at her plate now empty of the short ribs.

Jillian had been surprised to receive an invitation to the opening night of Gabriel's restaurant. Of course, she knew Cole had been behind it and had seen the look on

Nicolette's face when she'd arrived that his mother had been none too pleased. Nicolette Lavoie-Cress clearly didn't favor socializing with the help.

Tough.

She glanced over at the family's table in the center of the restaurant and caught Cole's warm gaze on her— or rather, them. She took a sip of her champagne with a smile before looking up at Lorenzo, who was standing beside her table.

"You look like you could use some company, Jillian," he said.

I must look as good as I feel in this dress.

Another shadow darkened her table. "Looks can be deceiving, Zo," Cole said.

Jillian frowned at the possessiveness of his tone.

Lorenzo nodded in understanding before turning to walk away.

The jazzy background music filled the silence.

"You crossed a line," she said, rising and picking up the sequined purse she'd picked to complement her red-satin wrap dress with its delicate spaghetti straps and a plunging neckline—a leftover from her time traveling the world. "Suddenly, this thing of ours has developed strings."

"Jillian—"

He reached for her arm, but she easily evaded his touch and walked away, clearly ready to leave the small, intimate restaurant with its clean, stylish décor of pale walls, dark furnishings and bronzed accents behind. She opened the copper-trimmed glass door and stepped out onto the street without looking back.

At the sight of Gabriel and Monica at the other end of the block sharing a kiss, she smiled before heading in the opposite direction toward her red Mazda Miata with its black-canvas convertible top.

"Let's go home, Cherry," she said before unlocking the door and giving it a hard jerk.

Once the restaurant failed, the flashy BMW she'd purchased during better days as a private chef was repossessed when the payments were more than she could handle. She had returned to driving the cute and sporty little Miata her parents purchased for her at eighteen. It was fifteen years old and a bit finicky at times. When the engine didn't start on the first try, she caressed the steering wheel and tried again. "Mama loves you," she whispered, easing onto the street.

The drive to her modest loft apartment in Brooklyn went well, and she was glad to pull into her parking spot in the garage. She quickly made her way to the elevator and up to the ninth floor. She loved the building's architecture: exposed brick, piping and ducts, beamed ceilings, wood columns and oversize windows. The blend of industrialized style with modern appliances and design gave it an aesthetic she had fallen in love with and had been pleased to be able to afford. She didn't have a lot of space, less than seven hundred square feet, but the ceilings were ten feet high, and the city's views were vibrant at night.

As soon as she unlocked her sliding metal barn door, Jillian began undressing, leaving a deliberate trail of sequined clutch, heels, flashy red-satin dress and then her panties. Nude, she walked across the hardwood floor to the kitchen to pour herself a glass of wine. She'd gotten all dolled up. Attended the event. Eaten delicious food. And now she was ready to relax.

Her front door slid open and Cole stepped inside, still handsome in his black suit and tie. Jillian took a deep sip of her wine. "What took you so long?" she asked with a glance over her shoulder.

He closed and locked the door, then came toward her with heated eyes as he undressed and dropped his clothing atop hers. "How were you so sure I was coming?" he asked, removing his boxers and kicking them away to slide across the polished hardwood.

Jillian gave him a look that said "puh-leeze" as she enjoyed the sight of his sculpted nude body. His inches, darker toned than the rest of him, grew in length before her eyes, with a slight lean to the right. And led him right over to her. She was already shivering in anticipation as he wrapped one strong arm around her waist and pulled her close to bury his face against her neck.

"Humph. You just wanted to make sure Lorenzo wasn't sniffing around," she teased.

He stiffened and raised his head to look down at her. "Really?" he asked in his deep voice.

She gave him a soft laugh before leaning back in his embrace and drizzling some of her wine across her breasts. "Thirsty?"

He bent his knees to tongue the moisture. "And hungry," he moaned against her soft flesh.

Jillian flushed with heat. "Cole," she gasped as she

blindly set the glass atop the counter before pressing her hands to the hard contours of his back.

When he raised her body with ease to bury his face against her cleavage, she wrapped her legs around his waist. The first feel of his crafty tongue against her nipples rushed them to hardness. He suckled one of the tight buds into his mouth and she released a sigh of pleasure from deep within as she rolled her hips.

Her entire body felt alive with their sexual chemistry. The pulse they created was not to be ignored or denied. And it had been that way over the last year without hesitation or deceleration.

Jillian clung to Cole as he carried her over to the center of the loft and the brown-leather sofa that also served as her bed when there was time to open it. There wasn't. Passions unleashed, they needed quenching.

Cole sat on the sofa with her straddling his lap. She brushed the curls from her face as he leaned his head back and eyed her. Her face. Her breasts. Her belly. The close-shaved mound of her intimacy. He massaged her hips and upper thighs as she took his hard inches in her hand to stroke. He grunted at her touch and rocked his hips forward.

"It's so hard," she whispered, enjoying his wince of pleasure.

"It aches," he admitted.

Jillian took one of his hands and pressed it down between her thighs. He cupped her. The curve of his palm pressed against her warm, pulsing bud as the tips of his fingers stroked her lips. Heat and electricity infused her. She cried out in sweet release as she rolled against his touch. Her grip on his inches tightened, evoking a wild cry of pleasure from him that gave her such immense joy.

He straightened and pressed kisses from her jawline up to her ear. "Watching you in that little red dress all night, and not being able to touch you, was pure hell, Jillian," he rasped.

She trembled.

"All I could think of was getting it off you and me inside you," he continued before sucking her earlobe.

She panted sharply.

"Did you have on a bra?" he asked.

She shook her head.

"I could tell."

He leaned her upper body back and lowered his head to lick her nipple and then caress it with a cool, steady stream of air.

"Damn," she swore with a gasp.

He switched his wicked onslaught to her other breast.

"That. Is. Amazing," Jillian admitted as he tended to her with slow and deliberate care.

She pressed her hand to his head and leaned to the right to open the wood box atop the square glass end table to retrieve one of the dozen condoms inside. She was ready for him. Wet, throbbing and in heat.

Tearing the foil, she removed the ribbed ultra-sensitive latex.

"You ready?" he asked, watching her work the protection along the length of his hard inches.

She nodded.

"I wanted to taste you the way you like," he said, his voice thick.

"*We* like," Jillian reminded him, rising on her knees.

"It's the best meal I've ever eaten," Cole said, his smile wicked.

"Really?" Jillian asked, easing onto him.

Slowly.

They stared into each other's eyes, mouths open at the feel of her tightness surrounding his hardness.

Cole swore as the thick base of his erection entered her.

She dropped her head back and looked up at the ceiling, feeling her eyes glaze over with passion. She took a moment to adjust to the feel of him pressing against her walls. He throbbed inside her. She liked it—a lot.

Cole pressed his hands to her back and pulled her forward to kiss her. First, a slow press of their lips, and then he deepened it with his tongue and a guttural moan as she rocked her hips back and forth. She ended each smooth glide with a Kegel that gripped and released him. He liked that—a lot.

With her hands pressed to the sides of his face and his arms wrapped around her so tightly that her breasts flattened against his hard chest, they slowly ground against each other as they took turns sucking each other's tongues. Sweat coated their bodies. She felt his heart pounding hard, just like her own. He lowered one arm to grip a handful of one of her round buttocks. She whimpered into his mouth.

"So good," he moaned, his eyes searching hers.

She nodded with urgency before she licked at his mouth and suckled his bottom lip. "Damn good," she agreed, stopping to clutch and release his inches with her walls.

"Jillian," he moaned, leaning back against the sofa and drawing her forward with him.

She rose slightly on her knees and took the lead in riding home. Nice and slow. Wicked and deliberate. She always wanted to give as good as she got, and the truth was that Cole Cress was *the* best lover she had ever had. Attentive. Passionate. Lengthy. It was nothing after a long night of numerous climaxes for her to beg him to claim his own happy ending to bring the passionate torture to an end. It was commonplace for them to sex each other to sleep and then have him wake her not long after for more.

His stamina was beyond impressive.

And addictive.

She broke the kiss to look at him with soft eyes and a hint of a smile. "I really like having sex with you," she whispered.

"Same," he agreed.

"And the best part," Jillian said, quickening the back-and-forth motion of her hips.

"What?"

"Climaxing while you're inside me."

She felt his tool stiffen.

"Same," he said, lifting his head to capture her mouth with his own.

Together they moved in unison, fast and hard, as they drove each other headfirst into the electrifying white-hot spasms of their climaxes. Moans. Hoarse cries. Hurried and frantic movements. Mindless falls into the hot abyss together. Shaken. Stirred.

With one last high-pitched cry, Jillian collapsed against him and rested her forehead against the top of the sofa as he rubbed her back and pressed kisses to her shoulder.

The aftermath of their fiery connection had them both sweaty and spent.

Ding-dong.

Jillian frowned at the sound as she raised her head.

"Not Leon I hope," Cole quipped, a teasing light in his electric eyes.

She sat upright and lightly pinched one of his nipples. "You're sexier than you are funny, Cress," she said, rising to walk over to the door where she kept a tablet on a small metal table in the corner. On the screen was the video feed from her doorbell. And she was looking at the face of Nicolette Cress.

"It's your mother," Jillian whispered, her heart pounding at the shock as she galvanized into action, picking up their trail of clothing.

Cole stood and deeply frowned. "What?" he asked.

Jillian gave him a dramatic shove as she took quick steps to the sofa and slapped the clothing against his chest. "Bathroom," she ordered.

"What!" he exclaimed, now holding the pile in his arms. "I'm not hiding from my mother."

She turned to open the engraved armoire against the wall to remove a cotton robe. "Yes, you are. Because I need my job, and your mother is not firing me because she discovered The Rebel naked—"

"The Rebel?" Cole scoffed.

"Yes," Jillian stressed as she pulled on the robe and moved to push him across the apartment.

Ding-dong.

Cole's frown deepened as he back-stepped into the bathroom. One of her sexy heels dropped from the heap in his arms.

Jillian motioned with her hand for him to back up some more so that she could grab the doorknob. "Two rings? Your mother's a little pushy," she said before pulling the door closed.

Cole set their clothing in the sink before easing the door open a little. Through the crack, he watched Jillian sniff the air and survey the scene. She suddenly jumped, as if frightened, and rushed over to the sofa. Picking up the empty condom wrapper, she slid it into the pocket of her bright yellow robe. He looked down at the latex still clinging to him, filled with his release.

"Mrs. Cress?" Jillian said, feigning surprise. "It's a little late, and I was running a bath."

"You and I need to speak," his mother said.

About what?

"I'm curious what we have to discuss that couldn't wait until I got to work in the morning," Jillian returned coolly.

Feisty.

Cole covered his mouth to trap a yawn. A night of decadent food and champagne capped off with mind-blowing sex, he wanted nothing more than to sleep it off. He leaned against the sink and crossed his arms over his chest as he listened to their conversation.

"Your dealings with my son," Nicolette said.

Cole stiffened.

"Excuse me," Jillian said. "You're mistaken."

He stepped closer to peek through the slit of the open bathroom door. His mother and his lover were facing each other. Jillian's back was to him. He grimaced as he fought the urge to dress and leave his hiding place to admonish his mother for dipping into his business.

Her hiring of Jillian as part of her household staff was Nicolette's business.

"Tonight, at Gabriel's, was very revealing when Lorenzo and Cole seemed to bump heads about you," Nicolette said, looking around at Jillian's apartment before casting her blue gaze squarely on the chef. "That, plus Cole unable to take his eyes off you in that red dress, was telling."

Just deny it, Jillian, and send her on her way so we can go to bed.

Jillian shook her head. "Mrs. Cress—"

His mother held up her hand to stop her. "I don't have time for games or pretenses," she said in her heavy French accent. "I know my sons. Probably better than they like. He wants you or has had you. Either way, I want it to end."

Cole frowned as he straightened to his full height. Anger burned the pit of his stomach. He couldn't believe what he was hearing.

"And if you end whatever it is you two have going on, I will appoint you an executive chef at one of the Cress restaurants…in another state," Nicolette finished. "So, choose. Either way, you are done at the townhouse. I won't pay you to screw my son."

What the hell?

This was a side of his mother Cole had never seen before. Cold. Manipulating. Controlling.

"But you will offer me an executive chef position instead?" Jillian countered with a tinge of sarcasm.

"The only talents of yours I am interested in my family enjoying are in the kitchen," Nicolette said.

"Mrs. Cress, I refuse to be insulted in my home. It can fit inside your pantry, but it's mine," Jillian asserted.

No nonsense until the end.

Nicolette chuckled. It was mocking. "And my son might fit inside you, but *he's* mine, and I do not want this thing between you to get out of hand."

He turned and dug through the pile of clothing for his underwear and suit pants. He was ready to confront his mother. "This is bull—"

He paused in jerking on his boxers at the sound of the front door sliding closed. He felt like a fool, frozen like a deer in headlights in Jillian's cramped bathroom, waiting to hear what was going on. He pulled his boxer briefs up, dropped the black pants, and opened the door to step out.

Jillian, locking the front door, glanced back over her shoulder. "She's gone, Cole."

"I figured that out since I was in the only hiding place in here," he said, standing with his hands on his hips.

She smiled at him as she crossed her arms over her chest and made her way to one of the three expansive arched windows of her apartment.

"I'm sorry about that, Jillian," he said. "I had no idea my mother would ever pull such a stunt."

"It's not your fault, Cole," she said, leaning against the window, the city's nightscape as her background.

He walked to her and wrapped an arm around her waist to pull her back against his body. "She left before I could set her straight about this stunt," he said, eyeing Jillian's reflection. "But I will as soon as I see her. I can't believe she insulted you like that."

He frowned at her continued silence.

"Cole—" Jillian raised her eyes to lock with his in the window "—I'm going to take the job."

His frown deepened as he stepped back, releasing her from his grasp. His jaw worked in rising irritation as he realized that Jillian was putting her ambition before him.

What was it she'd said at the restaurant? *Suddenly this thing of ours has developed strings.*

Right. They were never meant to last.

Although he and Traci had been in a relationship, Jillian's choice felt like a similar betrayal. Not as callously calculated as Traci's machinations...

Or was it?

She turned and leaned back against the window as she stared at him, asserting, "It's an opportunity that I can't pass up, Cole."

Still...

It stung.

He released a bitter chuckle and shook his head before turning to cross the room to enter the bathroom.

He dressed and made a conscious effort to not let his anger toss her clothing. That would be childish. He was sardonic at times and could find humor where most could not, but he wasn't silly. As he smoothed the lapels of his suit jacket, he eyed himself in the mirror above the sink. In the reflection, he saw the truth of his anger at Jillian.

And his hurt.

Cole cleared his throat and forced away the emotion lining his face.

It was not his first time looking betrayal in the face.

But it will be the last.

He left the bathroom. "Have a good life, Jillian," he said, taking long strides to the door.

She rushed across the space to stand in front of him. "Cole, talk to me," she urged, clenching his upper arms.

He brushed off her touch. "The way you did before you decided we were done without even talking to me?" His tone was so very cold.

"This was no strings, remember," she said. "We were just having fun. *Remember?*"

He looked down at her. "I'm clear about that," he

assured her. "I just didn't know you would use me for your come-up. Excuse me if that's hard to swallow."

She looked pained by his words. "It's so easy to speak from your seat of privilege, Cole," she said.

He scowled. "Privilege?" he barked.

"Your family. Cress, INC. Your wealth." She ticked off each on her fingers.

"None of those things earned me my first James Beard at just twenty, and you damn well know that— or you should, *Chef*," he said, letting his ire drip off the word.

"Don't mock me, Cole," Jillian said, her voice soft.

"Don't shortchange yourself," he shot back.

"What do you mean?"

"Why not gain the position based on your skill and not a payoff where you collude with my mother to control my damn life?" His voice was hard, unrelenting.

"You made a scene tonight, Cole. Your mother discovered our personal business because of you. I lost my job tonight, Cole," Jillian said, her hands slashing the air as she pointed at him.

True.

"Why can't you see this from my point of view? Get out of your hurt feelings and see the position I'm in?"

"Hurt feelings!" he charged. "This is anger. Disgust. Disappointment. Not hurt. No strings, remember?"

They both fell silent. Somehow it was filled with turbulence.

He turned from her and paced as he slid his hands into the pockets of his slacks. He'd look over at her, feel the stab of her betrayal, and look away. Mixed with his anger was confusion.

Why does this bother me so much?

The old Cole would have laughed, popped champagne, and celebrated her new position with her before one last "sexcapade" to carry him through the dry spell until he met his next no-strings attachment.

Foolishly, there had been moments over the last year when he'd felt his time with Jillian was different, but he'd ignored them. Still, she was not his forever. He'd known that going in, and she'd made it clear as it came to a shattering end.

"Cole," Jillian called over to him.

He looked at her. Her robe puddled at her feet, she stood naked before him. Just as beautiful, alluring and tempting as ever. His body betrayed him and he began to harden. It would be easy to narrow the space between them, hitch her against the door, and fill her until he climaxed.

So very easy.

But things were different. His trust in her had been shattered. And if there was one thing he'd learned from life, it was that trust was everything to him.

"You made your choice, Jillian," he said, his voice low as he treated his eyes to one last intimate look at her body. A playground he had enjoyed with relish over the last year. He would miss it. "I wouldn't want you to go back on your word to my mother. Besides, your debt to my family and me is well paid."

Jillian gasped at the dig as she raced to him and slapped him soundly at the implied insult.

Whap!

It turned his head to the left. It stung. But not as deeply as the ache radiating across his chest. Or the betrayal he felt at himself for hating that he'd sunk low enough to insult her in such a manner. Still, he bit his bottom lip to keep from apologizing and instead breezed past her to leave the apartment and Jillian behind.

Three

Two months later

"Your new apartment is beautiful, Jillie."

Jillian turned her phone from her waterfront view in San Francisco to look at her family on the screen via FaceTime. Her father, Harry Rossi—whom she favored— her mother, Nora—from whom she got her humor—and her grandmother, Ionie. They were all huddled in front of the computer in Rochester, New York, in her parents' home.

"Thank you, Gram," she said, taking a seat on the L-shaped sofa as she eyed the petite senior with her short silver curls and her beloved fuchsia lipstick. She was vibrant, smart, and funny, but the grandmother she knew was beginning to fade a bit as a chronic heart condition weakened her.

Jillian fought the urge to ask her how she was doing, knowing it irritated her to be coddled.

"We miss you, Jillie, but we're proud of you," Harry said in a booming voice that matched his lofty broad frame.

Her mother lovingly called him Bear.

And their love, since the days they'd been in high school, was sickeningly adorable. Arguments were few and far between. Shows of affection were often. Lots and lots of laughter. Long hugs. And slow dances with whispered promises.

They loved and liked each other.

That was her childhood.

It was her search for her own "Mr. Right" or "The One" or her "happily-ever-after" that had led to Jillian's two failed marriages. The first at just eighteen to Warren Long, her high school sweetheart. A wedding at the county courthouse and a year of arguing over their lack of money as they both attended college made them realize they were too young—and had moved too fast—to be married. Thankfully once the hurt and bitterness had faded, they'd remained in touch over the years.

That had not been the case with her second husband, Chuckie Forge. They'd met when she'd been hired as a line cook in his small but popular restaurant in the Hell's Kitchen section of Manhattan. Their fiery, passionate three-month affair had led to a Vegas marriage that had crashed and burned when he'd disappeared for an entire weekend with his pastry chef. Unlike Warren, Jillian disdained Chuckie and was pleased to never lay eyes on him again.

"How are things going with the restaurant?" Her father's question interrupted her musings.

"Better," she said. "The shift between being a personal chef and an executive chef for a restaurant that is part of a brand is huge for me. There's less freedom."

"You understand that. Right?" her father asked.

"Absolutely," she assured him.

And she did. But still, she wished she could plan the menu without input from corporate or restaurant management. It felt formulaic, and she suspected it was why the position had been left open following the previous chef's exit. He now operated his own restaurant.

Her grandmother covered her mouth with a yawn. Jillian smiled. The three-hour time difference was taking some getting used to, as well. It was six in California, but on the East Coast it was nine at night. Definitely past her grandmother's bedtime.

But she wasn't ready to say good-night to them.

She was lonely.

Jillian looked past the phone to her spacious furnished apartment with its incredible waterfront views and just a walk from the restaurant, CRESSIII. Her new six-figure salary would pay off her debt within a year. And the press generated by Cress, INC.'s public relations team of her hire as executive chef might lead to even more opportunities.

None of it replaced the surprising hole left in her life without Cole.

She sighed.

"Everything okay, Jillie?" Ionie asked, leaning closer to the screen.

Jillian smiled when her grandmother tapped it. "I'm not frozen, Gram," she said.

"Oh. Okay," Ionie said. "I can't be right and hit it out of the park all the time to bat a thousand."

Ionie *loved* the New York Mets.

"Listen, Jillie, my bed is calling my name," she said, standing. "And I'm going to answer. Videophone me tomorrow."

"It's FaceTime, Mom," Harry said with a playful wink at the screen as his mother turned and walked away.

Ionie was filled with one-liners and it never took much to nudge one out of her.

"Tomato to*ma*to, Harry. Same difference, son," she called over her shoulder as she sauntered away with a sway of her hips.

They all chuckled.

The eighty-year-old retired schoolteacher was a spitfire. They adored her.

"How is she doing?" Jillian asked.

"Better. The full-time nurse is great with both of us working," Harry said.

"We worry a lot less about her being home alone, so the *nurse* is a huge help," her mom told her. "And thank you for your help with the cost, Jillie. I'm proud of you for taking on that responsibility."

"No worries. We're family. It's what we do," she assured them.

"Why aren't you at work?" Nora asked as she licked the tip of her thumb and swiped at something on her husband's cheek.

"The restaurant is closed on Mondays," she explained, fighting the urge to rub her eyes since she was wearing her contacts.

Her brow furrowed when her father pressed a kiss to her mother's palm and they shared a look.

Jillian moaned, having seen that look a million times during her childhood and knowing a kiss was next. Just sickeningly sweet.

"Let me let y'all go," she said, zooming her finger in on the button to end the call.

"Bye," they said in unison just before the screen went black.

She released a heavy breath and dropped her phone onto the sofa. The silence of the apartment echoed. She leaned forward to pick up the remote from the leather ottoman serving as a coffee table to turn on the wall-mounted television.

Nothing held her attention.

And everything seemed to remind her of Cole.

A romantic movie where the couple shared a kiss.

Cole was an excellent kisser.

She switched the channel.

Click, click.

A commercial for soap.

Jillian smiled, remembering them squeezing into her small tub together to share a bubble bath.

She frowned and raised the remote.

Click, click.

A weather news story about a string of rainy days ahead.

I remember that weekend at my apartment when we stayed inside, cooked for each other, and had the most amazing rainy-day sex.

She shook her head to clear it of the steamy memories.

Click, click.

This time she turned the television off. She couldn't escape her thoughts of *him*. Cole. Cole. Cole. Cole.

She looked down at her phone.

Don't do it. Move on. You made your choice. Live with it. And stay off his Instagram.

Jillian pushed aside her thoughts and snatched up her phone. Her heart pounded, and she felt nervous butterflies as she scrolled through his feed. He hadn't posted in weeks.

She paused at a photo of him leaning against his high-end food truck. Serious face. Electric eyes in his brown complexion. All-black attire. Sexy as sexy could be.

I miss him.

The nights were the worst. They used to tease it was their "sexing hours." Jillian had lost count of those after-midnight hours where one would text the other. Within the hour, he would arrive and, not long after he was hard, she was wet, and their grunts of pleasure echoed in her loft apartment. On the door. The floor. The shower. The sofa—open and closed. Against the window.

She bit her bottom lip and closed her eyes with a deep moan at the visual of his hard buttocks clenching and unclenching as he stroked inside her, her back and buttocks pressed against the windows. Her knees had clutched his sides and her fingers had dug into his shoulders as he'd delivered one deep thrust after another.

I could use Cole's special delivery.

But those days—and nights—were over, and her body was going through withdrawal.

Over the last couple of months, had she second-guessed ending her dalliance with Cole? Yes. But in those moments, she reminded herself forever had never been a part of their plans. Still, she had never intended for him to feel offended or put off.

Jillian had tried a few times in the weeks following her rushed moved to San Francisco to call him, but he'd never answered. She'd wanted to get it through to him that the hefty salary would allow her to assist her parents with the expensive medical care her grandmother required, to say nothing of help clear the hefty debt from her first restaurant closing. Her duty to her family and her success was interwoven—it had to be.

Wealth was not a part of her legacy.

Unlike Cole.

And now her life was moving on.

Without Cole.

Within the year, her feelings for the sexy rebel had deepened beyond just a fling. Hindsight was always twenty-twenty because that realization hadn't hit home until he'd been out of her life for good. She had thought she'd only wanted sex from him, but she ached with sadness for more than that, wanting to hear his deep voice, to make him laugh with her dry wit, or to have him surprise her with one of his notes.

Jillian rose from the sofa and made her way to her bedroom. On her bedside table was the carved wood box from her loft in New York. She opened it. Gone were the condoms. Instead it held every monogrammed note Cole had ever given her over the last year. It wasn't until she'd packed up her things that she'd found them all randomly placed around her apartment. In a cookbook. Mixed with mail. In the back pocket of jeans.

Anywhere and everywhere. She'd never thrown them away.

She sat on the edge of the bed and picked up the box, holding it up to her nose. The scent of his crisp cologne still clung to some of the notes. She smiled a little as she opened each folded card.

Some were funny.

"'What's black and white and hard all over?'" she read, chuckling at his play on his mixed-race heritage and his desire for her.

Most were steamy.

"'There is nothing better than the taste of you,'" she read, letting her finger stroke his slashing handwritten words.

She had taken the notes for granted.

As she sat with Cole's notes scattered on her lap, she fast realized she had taken the time they'd shared for granted, as well.

Bzzzzzz. Bzzzzzz. Bzzzzzz.
Cole ignored his cell phone vibrating in the inner pocket of his black tuxedo jacket as he placed his small stack of hundred-dollar chips on the roulette table of

the luxurious, historic casino in Monte Carlo, Monaco. He kept his eyes on the ball after the dealer waved his hand across the table, signaling no more bets. He took a sip from his snifter of whiskey and, with a calm aloofness, watched the ball fall onto the winning number.

He smiled as the dealer pushed a sizable stack of chips next to his on the number four. "Luck be *my* lady tonight," he said, playing on the lyrics of the 1950's Frank Sinatra song.

"Then call me Luck."

Cole was waiting for the dealer to pay out all winners on the board. He looked to his right at the sultry feminine voice and found a beautiful, svelte woman offering him an alluring smile. Her skin was the color of dark chocolate. The crimson she wore on her lips and her body was electrifying. From her accent and the high cut of her cheekbones, he assumed she was of African descent—a regal beauty with the type of style that spoke of elegance and wealth.

He felt annoyance that he instantly compared her to Jillian. Two months later and thoughts of her still replayed on a loop in his mind.

"You've been here for a month, and you're always alone. It's time for you to make a new friend," the sultry beauty said, drawing his attention once again. She extended her hand. "Lesedi Osei."

He took her hand into his own. "Cole Cress," he said, easing out of their shake when her finger pressed against his inner wrist.

Before Jillian, he would have matched Lesedi's vibe, offered her an early morning breakfast as the clock struck four in the morning, and then taken her to his bed to make sure she never regretted her boldness in approaching him.

He retrieved all of his tokens before turning to her. "And if you know I've been here that long, then so have you," he said.

She tucked a metallic leather clutch under her arm. It matched the strapless minidress she wore. "My family is staying in Monte Carlo for the summer," she said, her accent giving her voice a lilting quality.

"Nigerian?" he asked of her heritage.

"Very good," she said with an incline of her head.

He watched her tuck her shoulder-length bob behind her ear and glance away. A flirty move that was subtle. He caught it. She was interested.

Am I?

He eyed her. But it was Jillian's shapely frame in the dress that he saw.

That angered him.

To be intimate with this beautiful chocolate woman before him would be nothing more than using her to relieve his sexual frustration and make him forget a woman whose past betrayal stung like it happened yesterday.

Damn.

Lesedi looked up at him with a regretful smile. "Whoever she is, she is truly the lucky one," she said.

"She doesn't deserve it," he mumbled, clenching his jaw.

Lesedi opened her clutch and removed a business card to extend to him between her index and middle finger. "*If* you ever fix it or forget it…" she said before walking past him with one soft pat to his chest.

As he slid the card into the front pocket with his phone, he turned and watched her walk away before she disappeared into the crowd. Deciding his night of gambling, drinks and fine food was done, Cole left the elaborately decorated casino to take the stairs up to the hotel lobby. Here, too, the architecture spoke to its long history and grandeur.

Last month he had been at the family's country estate in Paris when the house staff made his mother aware that he was staying there. Once her incessant calls bounced between his cell and the estate's landline, Cole had caught the first flight to Monte Carlo. Within hours, he'd been safely tucked away in the city of glamour, enjoying the serene quiet of the days and the endless opportunities of an active nightlife.

As he caught the elevator to his suite, he pulled his cell phone from his pocket. He wasn't surprised to see his mother's number. Nicolette Cress was on a mission to bring the wandering son back into the fold. She was huge on the family remaining close.

Thus, the townhouse large enough…for them all.

Same as the business…for them all.

Nicolette was so intent on family unity that she'd mediated Gabriel's part-time return to Cress, INC. as he'd put his primary focus on his restaurant and she'd capitulated on his relationship with Monica, the family's former maid.

Where Phillip Senior was stern in his demand for family loyalty, Nicolette used a different approach—

knowing how to sway all the men in her life to bend at her will.

The night he saw his mother move with such calculating coldness for his feelings at Jillian's apartment, he had never returned to the Cress townhouse. He'd spent the night at a hotel in Midtown Manhattan and flown to Paris the next day. He kept in touch with his brothers to assure his mother that he was alive and well, but he had, thus far, avoided any direct communication with her and handled his business decisions via Zoom calls and emails.

No one knew that Jillian was at the root of his annoyance with his mother.

Cole entered his deluxe suite. With the linen curtains of the terrace door open, the moon cast the room's modern décor with light. The shades of white, powder blue and taupe matched the view of the sea. It was calming by day or night.

He kicked off his handmade leather shoes, undid the top buttons of his shirt and unlatched the band of his Piaget watch as he crossed the marbled entryway to make his way down the hall to the bedroom. His yawn was hard to deny because of the late hour, but he walked up the space between the all-white, king-size bed and the sitting area's suede chair to open the terrace door. The scent of the sea reached him. The sight of the moon's rays glistening upon the waters calmed him as he took in the views of the city's Belle Époque architecture among the surrounding green hills.

It was too magnificent to ignore.

And he could use the tranquility.

Thoughts of Jillian made him feel as if a storm was brewing inside him with no escape. He missed her. That truth caused him to clench his teeth and release a heavy breath filled with his frustration at her.

And himself.

He felt like a fool.

Cole walked back into the suite to pour himself two fingers of whiskey from the crystal decanter on the bar in the sitting area's corner. With a sip, he made his way back onto the terrace. In truth, he avoided slumber because she conquered his sleeping hours—through dreams and nightmares.

Had he known the first time he'd laid eyes on the beauty that it would end the way it had, he never would have made the first move that day…

Cole and his brothers were in the movie room on the second floor of the five-story townhouse. It was a rare night that they all were home, and when the youngest Cress family member requested that they watch her favorite animated movie, Moana, her wishes were the command of the family. She was everyone's soft spot as the inner struggle to be named heir to the Cress, INC. throne reigned.

Cole had been the last to come down from his bedroom suite on the fourth floor. Everyone was seated in one of the twenty leather recliners that faced the movie screen. Collette sat front and center, her cup-holders filled with snacks—a treat because her mother always plied her with healthy alternatives.

"Hurry, Uncle Cole," she urged, her cheeks stuffed with candy.

Cole moved to the fully stocked snack station along the far wall, next to the entry to the wrought-iron staircase. It was completely stocked with a variety of boxed candy, a popcorn maker, a soda fountain and an ice cream machine. He selected a box of Goobers from the stack on the glass shelves. "Where's Mom?" he asked before opening the box and tossing a few of the treats into his mouth.

"She's interviewing the new chef," Phillip Senior said, kicking the recliner back and elevating his feet.

"Oh yeah?" Cole said. "Franco will be hard to top."

Their chef of the last ten years had retired with plans to return to his native Brazil. His traditional dishes had impressed the family of chefs. Even Phillip Senior had begrudgingly admitted that Franco's feijoada—a Brazilian beef, pork and bean stew—was better than his own.

Who would top that? he wondered.

Curious, Cole moved to the tablet on the wood-paneled wall and accessed the house's security system. Every room of the townhouse was under surveillance. Except, of course, his parents' suite, which took up the entire third floor and the six personal bedroom suites on the fourth and fifth floors.

He found his mother in the living room, seated on the light gray velvet sofa across from a young woman on the other.

She sat with poise and confidence in a stylish black pantsuit, her ankles crossed as she looked his mother *directly in the eye. Her curly hair had been pulled into a topknot and her spectacles were perched on her nose. With her plump lips covered in red lipstick, he couldn't help but think she had the air of a naughty librarian waiting to be untamed.*

"Cole, close the curtains and kill the lights," Lucas called over to him.

Cole forced his eyes away from the woman's face to look over at the second half of the spacious floor that made up the library with its floor-to-ceiling shelves lined with books. Like the other four floors of the townhouse, the entire rear wall was glass. He used the button on the light switch by the stairwell to close the soft gray velvet curtains. He dimmed the lights as well, just as the movie started. Although night and its darkness reigned, his actions would ensure a better movie-watching experience.

Instead of claiming a seat, however, he used the darkness to descend the wrought-iron staircase. It opened directly into the first-floor living room, but he paused, crossed his arms and leaned against the railing to watch the stranger from across the room.

She was beautiful. Her voice husky. Her confidence clear.

"I'll be honest, Jillian, I am very impressed by your previous employers," Nicolette said.

Jillian.

"I am very interested in someone used to decorum and discretion," his mother continued.

"Of course," Jillian agreed with a nod just before

*she glanced past his mother's shoulder to look at him.
Her eyes widened slightly in surprise.*

*He gave her his best smile—the one that had wooed
many a woman over the years. Nice, easy, and charming, with the right amount of wile.*

*Jillian shifted her eyes back to his mother, but he
saw the spark of interest before she did.*

*It made his pulse race, and he felt excited in a way
that surprised him. He decided right then that he
wanted Jillian, and he would charm the beauty right
into his bed...*

And he had.

And it had been glorious. Never had he had so much
fun in a pantry.

Cole pushed away the hot memory. As he stood on
the terrace of his suite in Monte Carlo, nursing her betrayal and his drink, he understood the chorus from the
song *I Wish* by Carl Thomas because he wished he'd
never met Jillian Rossi at all.

He felt used by her.

True, their relationship had been casual, but he'd
still thought it had meant more to her than something
to toss away without a second thought after more than
a year of sharing time.

Bzzzzzz. Bzzzzzz. Bzzzzzz.

Cole eased his phone from his inner pocket again. It
was Gabe. It was just after nine thirty on the East Coast.
His family had no way of knowing they were reaching
out to him at odd hours where he was.

He answered the call. "Yeah?" he said.

"Hey, stranger."

He chuckled before he took another deep sip of his drink. "How can I help you, big brother?" he drawled to the man who was older than him by two years.

They'd grown up close and had remained so in their adult years.

"Asking just what spurned this journey you're on would be a waste of time, I guess?" Gabe asked.

Cole's grip on his glass tightened. Usually, he and Gabe were honest with each other. In fact, Gabe was the only family member who knew of his relationship with Jillian. He knew his brother would keep whatever secrets he'd shared with him, but he was hesitant to share just how much Jillian's and their mother's actions had angered and disturbed him.

"If you sneaked off to San Francisco, believe me, I understand," Gabe assured him.

Cole frowned as he sat on one of the lounge chairs. "San Francisco?" he asked.

"To be with Jillian."

Cole's gut clenched.

So that's where she is.

He had made it his business to avoid knowing Jillian's whereabouts. Out of New York was more than enough. "We're done," he said, his voice sounding cold even to his ears.

"You want to talk about it?"

She used ending things with me as a stepping stone for her career.

He could still feel her heel in his back.

"Nah," Cole said with a shake of his head even though his brother couldn't see him.

"You sure?"

"Yes," he admitted with a begrudging smile.

The line went quiet.

"Gabe?" Cole wondered if the call had ended.

"One sec," Gabe said, sounding distracted.

Cole knew his brother well, and Gabe was a thinker. That's what made him the best choice to take over as CEO of Cress, INC.—if he hadn't already turned down the position. "Leave it alone, Gabe," he warned, knowing he was putting the pieces to the puzzle together.

"You're not speaking to Mom, who pushed for Jillian's new executive chef position..."

Cole jumped to his feet. "Gabe," he snapped.

"Okay, okay." He acquiesced. "Listen, I called because I need you to attend the Chef Gala."

Every year Cress, INC. held a glitzy dinner party for all the chefs from across the country. Gabe served as the president of the restaurant division, and this event was essential to his brother. But it would put Cole directly in the room with the two women he was avoiding—Jillian and his mother.

"No," Cole said firmly.

"Listen, Monica and I are announcing our engagement. I *need* you there," Gabe stressed.

They had been brothers for thirty years. Never had they not had each other's back. Not once. And there had been plenty of times that Gabe had saved the behind of his rebellious teenage brother hell-bent on wreaking havoc.

Cole released a long breath before turning to make his way inside his suite to replenish his drink.

"I'll be there," he promised.

Four

He really hates me.

Jillian took a deep sip of champagne as she stared across the original CRESS restaurant at Cole. When she'd walked into the Midtown Manhattan restaurant filled with nerves but still feeling beautiful in her elegant attire, she never assumed his anger was still so visceral that he would barely glance at her when their paths crossed.

It was as if she hadn't existed.

"Hello, Cole," she'd said with a smile.

"Jillian," was his cold and clipped response as he'd barely broken his stride past her.

It hadn't helped that he'd looked dark and sexy in his tuxedo with a crisp haircut and groomed shadow of beard. Just a gorgeous man. With an equally devastatingly fit body. She remembered it well.

"Jillian! It's so good to see you!"

She shifted her gaze to find Monica walking toward her in a white satin gown that fit her curvy frame like a second glove. "Wow. Love and lots of money suit you. You look gorgeous," she exclaimed as they shared a hug.

They'd both served at the pleasure of the Cress family as chef and maid. During that time, they had been friendly but not close. Still, it was good to see her. And in that moment of nursing hurt feelings because her former lover had treated her as a stranger; Jillian could use a friendly hug.

"You're the one. I love this," Monica said.

She stepped back to eye Jillian from her upswept curls to her sheer black, exposed-corset bustier draped with black-sequined fabric across her breasts and around her waist to trail down one leg of the satin palazzos she'd paired with the daringly risqué top.

"Thank you," Jillian said, trying to forget she'd wondered what Cole's reaction would be to her ensemble when she'd selected it last week from an exclusive women's boutique in San Francisco.

All for nothing.

"Congratulations on the new position," Monica said, stopping one of the uniformed waiters who passed by with a tray of flutes filled with vintage champagne.

Jillian remained silent to the praise. Her eyes had locked on a beautiful redhead with reality-defying breasts, uplifted by the bodice of her strapless emerald-green dress, saunter up to Cole and press a kiss to his cheek. She wound her arm around his. The move was clingy and possessive.

"Ohhhhh," Monica said, drawing the word out.

Jillian glanced over at her. "What?" she asked, feeling her heart pound.

"So, it was Cole with the naughty note of the 'taste of you lingering on his tongue'?" Monica asked with a sly look before taking another sip of her champagne.

Last year, Monica had been cleaning the kitchen and found one of Cole's sexy notes in Jillian's monogrammed cutlery bag. When she'd attended her first event with Gabe at the Cress townhouse as his girlfriend—surprising everyone including Jillian—she had asked which of the Cress men had written the note. Jillian had kept the truth a secret.

Until now.

"What gave it away?" Jillian asked.

"The look you just gave Cole and Kimber," Monica said. "So, I assume you kept your word of it ending once you left your job at the Cress townhouse."

Silly of me. "Something like that," Jillian said.

"Well, this should be good because the last thing Nicolette wants strutting around a Cress, INC. event is a woman with low IQ and high hem," Monica said.

"I'm sure he's just fine with both," Jillian drawled, chancing another look across the restaurant.

They weren't in the same spot.

CRESS, the first of the group of restaurants started by Cress, INC., was a beautiful, massive restaurant in hues of chrome and ivory with modern detailing and lots of lighting. A true showpiece.

Having been flown to New York, executive chefs from all eleven Cress restaurants had been put up in suites at a nearby five-star hotel. Phillip Senior and Nicolette were preparing a decadent seven-course meal for the gala dinner. It was a Monday and, with the restaurants closed, it was the perfect night to celebrate and motivate their chefs.

As she looked around the small crowd, Jillian was impressed by the attendees, including the stunningly handsome Lorenzo León Cortez. He looked so gorgeous in his light gray tux, matching silk tee and Native American neckpiece of black-braided leather and chunky turquoise. His long hair was pulled back from his handsome face.

"He is exquisite," Jillian said, remembering Cole being bothered by Lorenzo's attention to her the night of Gabe's restaurant opening.

"Zo?" Monica asked. "He's Gabe's best friend, so I plead the fifth."

"You could have just said he's not exquisite," Jillian reminded her.

"I'm not built to lie," Monica said, giving her a little wave before walking away with a wink.

Jillian cleared her throat and pressed her free hand to her belly before easing through the multitude of people toward Zo, who was standing at the L-shaped bar. He turned and did a double-take as she approached. She gave him a beguiling smile. He gave her a curious look.

Two can play Cole's game.

"Hello, Lorenzo," she said, looking up at his towering height.

He took a sip of his beer and eyed her with amusement. "Can I assume from the stares Cole is shooting at us that you're over here to make him jealous?" His deep voice seemed to rumble.

Jillian instantly felt childish and rightfully so. "Yes," she admitted, leaning her elbows against the edge of the bar.

Lorenzo chuckled as he bent a bit at the waist. "It worked," he said before walking away.

Moments later, she felt heightened awareness—like a shiver. She knew before Cole stood beside her that he was there.

"What games are you playing?" he asked.

The cool scent of his cologne teased her.

"So now you know me?" she asked before taking a sip of her champagne.

"I never knew you to play games, Jillian, but then I realized too late I never knew you at all," he said, his voice low enough for just her ears and cold enough to chill her to the bone.

Sadness waved over her, but she stiffened her spine and turned sideways to face his profile.

He's so damn handsome. And I miss him. I want him. I... I... I...

Jillian gasped at the realization of the depth of her feelings for Coleman Cress.

I love him.

Cole turned his head to look at her.

Their eyes met. She shivered and had to close her eyes to break the connection before her feelings for him tumbled from her mouth.

I love you, Cole.

"Jillian?"

The sound of her name on his lips was her undoing. She opened her eyes to turn and walk away from him as fast as she could on her heels without falling. Her heart beat faster. Her pulse sped up.

Missing him? Desiring him? Wanting to sex him? Fine.

Falling in love?

That was not a part of the plan.

Jillian reached the door to the hall leading to the restrooms. She paused at the entry and looked over her shoulder, still trembling from her revelation. Cole's date was back at his side, but his eyes were on her across the restaurant.

With intensity.

I love him.

She turned quickly and raced down the hall, her hand on the wall, to reach the ladies' room. As soon as she entered, she pushed the door closed and leaned against it for a few moments before moving to the sink to grip the edge of the counter. She studied her reflection. She felt afraid and excited.

Her breathing labored. Her heart pounded. Her pulse raced.

Just like that, *everything* had changed. Absolutely everything.

Damn.

Cole took a deep sip of his coffee with Kahlúa as he sat back in his seat at the line of tables set up for a family-style dinner for twenty-six guests. His parents sat side by side at one end, with Phillip Junior and Raquel at the other end. He looked along the table's length, elaborately decorated with floral arrangements and candles, at Jillian enjoying a conversation with Xin Lao, the executive chef of CRESS VIII in the Napa Valley.

She glanced up and he shifted his gaze away from her.

Earlier, at the bar, something had happened.

He'd seen a shift in Jillian's eyes, and it had shaken his soul. As she'd rushed away, he'd had to fight the instinctive urge to follow her. Stop her. Question her.

Kiss her.

His gut clenched.

When she'd paused at the entrance to the hall and looked back, he hadn't been able to take his eyes off her—and had struggled to stand firmly in place. When she'd turned to disappear down the hall, he'd felt regret.

Jillian Rossi was still in his system.

The first sight of her entering the restaurant in that strapless, almost revealing bustier with the wide-legged pants that emphasized her thick thighs, hips and rounded buttocks had him hungering for her. She was spectacular, and it had taken an Oscar-worthy performance for him to do nothing more than speak her name and move past her with a quickness when he'd first laid eyes on her.

All night, as his date had clung to him like Velcro, he'd watched Jillian without appearing to do so—something he'd learned during her days working in the family townhouse. He missed nothing. Every smile. Every laugh. Every introduction to a new person. Every handshake.

His desire and disdain for her battled deep within him.

"Cole? You okay?"

Kimber Locke drew his attention. He looked over at the Playboy model sitting beside him. Beautiful woman. Even pleasant to be around. Her role? To annoy his mother.

His parents had been busy preparing the elaborate meal for the night when he'd arrived. Once they'd stepped from the kitchen, free of their chef coats and in their designer evening wear, Cole had gently guided Kimber by her elbow through the crowd and into the direct line of vision of his parents. His mother's look had quickly shifted from surprise and pleasure at seeing him to fighting hard not to reveal her disgust at seeing Kimber at his side. Nicolette's private persona was different from the public one she'd carefully cultivated. For a brief moment, that façade cracked.

Nicolette Cress hated it when one of her sons paraded a nighttime liaison—especially at a business function.

"Yeah, I'm good. Thanks," he said.

Kimber gave him a conspiratorial wink. She was in on his hijinks. They'd briefly dated a few years ago, and she was well aware that her very presence irked his mother—making the ploy all the more enjoyable for her, as well.

The night was coming to an end. A decadent meal of French cuisine relished. A dessert of individual fruit tarts with different selections of exotic fruits devoured.

His parents' formal speech given, Gabe and Monica's engagement announcement celebrated. The annual bonus checks much appreciated.

But beneath the jovial surface, hell was brewing—and every Cress family member knew it.

Ding, ding, ding.

Cole turned his head to eye his parents rise from their seats to his left. He covered his mouth to hide his humor at his mother, fervently avoiding looking in his and Kimber's direction. Avoidance by Nicolette Cress was top-tier hidden anger.

"We want to thank you all for joining us tonight and allowing us to cook for you," Phillip Senior said with a broad smile.

Cole stared down into his cup of coffee. His father really could charm.

"Under the guidance of Gabriel and his team and the entire staff at Cress, INC., we thank you for providing the most important element—cooking delicious food," Phillip Senior continued. "Without your skill and love of food, Cress, INC. would not have had its most successful year to date."

Applause filled the air.

Cole looked up as his mother cast a beautiful smile at her husband. It was filled with love. He eyed his father bend from his tall height to kiss her.

Scoundrel.

Cole was angry at his mother for her machinations in his love life, but she was his mother and still deserving of his father's loyalty.

"Thank you all again. Have a good night. And safe travels in the morning back to your homes," Phillip said.

"If my family could just remain behind for a quick *bavardage*," Nicolette added, with an inadvertent glance at Cole before she forced a stiff smile.

Bavardage. The beautiful French word for chitchat, which she truly meant as "verbal lashing."

His parents and Gabe moved to the door to personally say goodbye as the chefs and their dates began to exit. Cole's eyes immediately went to Jillian as she tucked her clutch under her arm and made her way to the front. She didn't look at him.

He clenched his jaw, feeling dismissed and forgotten by her once again.

"Should I go?" Kimber asked.

"Definitely not," Cole said, watching as Jillian shook the hand of his mother and father before leaving.

Just outside the door, she paused and looked back over her bared shoulders. Their eyes met.

She gave him a hesitant smile, and his body betrayed him by desiring her in a rush.

His mother closed the door, breaking the connection. He eyed her, not doubting she had done it purposely.

Monte Carlo is calling my name.

Phillip Senior walked over to the bar and poured himself a Scotch.

His mother leaned against the door, released a heavy breath, and finally landed her cobalt eyes on him. Hard and intense.

They matched his own.

Her unspoken message to her son was clear. *Send her away or I will obliterate her.*

His mother's anger was nuclear and he knew Kimber's feelings would suffer collateral damage.

Cole leaned over. "Thanks for tonight. I owe you," he whispered near her ear.

Kimber smiled at him and pressed her hands to his cheeks as she tilted her head to kiss him. Deeply. And with a loud moan.

Cole fought not to laugh as she broke the kiss. She cleaned his mouth of her gloss with her thumb and then rose to walk away with sultry stride meant to annoy his mother.

Nicolette looked like she could spit bullets as she crossed her arms at her chest and moved away from the door with angry steps that sent her rose-gold evening gown fluttering behind her.

"I'll be waiting up for you, Cole," Kimber said with a wink and another blown kiss.

Nicolette released a cry and turned quickly to steer Kimber out the door before closing it.

He covered his mouth with his hand as he looked around the restaurant at his family members' expressions.

Phillip Junior looked pleased though his wife cast him an annoyed glare.

Sean had joined their father at the bar.

Gabe and Monica shared a look—she was clearly surprised by her first inclusion behind the Cress family veil.

Lucas was eyeing the fruit tart he'd ignored earlier.

Nobody wanted to be there.

"Bienvenue, Coleman. Je vois que tu as eu le temps de ramasser les poubelles," Nicolette said coldly in her native tongue.

Welcome back, Coleman. I see you had time to pick up the trash. He shook his head at her judgment.

"Kimber is not trash," he said, reaching for the anger that sent him away from his family for months. "And neither was Jillian."

Nicolette stiffened. "What do you mean?"

Cole rose to his full height. "I was at Jillian's that night. In the bathroom. I heard everything. I know what you did," he said, enjoying the widening of her eyes with each word he spoke.

Silence reigned.

"What's going on?" Phillip Senior asked from behind him.

"Jillian?" Lucas asked. "Nice, Cole. *Real* nice."

Cole ignored his brother's praise as he came to stand in front of his mother and look down at her. "The last thing I needed was for you to interfere in my life," he said. "It was a side of you I had never seen before, and I *never* want to see again. You judged Monica. You judged Jillian. It's time you sit down before a mirror and take a long hard look at yourself."

Nicolette's eyes filled with tears. "Cole," she whispered.

He shook his head, his eyes ablaze and his jaw firm. "What you did was wrong and deplorable—"

"That's enough, Cole," his father said, moving to wrap his arm around his wife's shoulders.

He ignored him. "We are your sons. We're grown men. We can decide on our own without you pulling strings like Geppetto," he continued.

"I only want what's best for you." Nicolette extended her arm to reach for his hand.

He pulled back from her touch. "Who says you know what's best?" he asked. "You don't even know what's best for you."

Nicolette's forehead wrinkled in confusion.

Cole shook his head and shifted past her to open the front door to the restaurant. "Kimber is waiting for me," he lied, leaving them all to ponder just what he'd meant.

Jillian looked at the two wedding photos she held. In both, she was so young.

And so naïve.

"Hey, you."

She looked up at her father standing in the doorway in T-shirt and pajama bottoms. They both looked over at Ionie, still asleep in her bed. "I wanted to be near her since I leave in the morning," Jillian admitted from where she sat on the rocking chair. She set the photos on her lap to reach over and lightly stroke her grandmother's soft silver curls.

Harry walked into the room and came to stand at the other side of the bed. "Yeah, I check on her every night before we go to bed," he admitted, talking low so as not to interrupt his mother's sleep.

Jillian gave him a soft smile. Her father was an only child raised by a single mother. His love for Ionie was boundless. She knew it was hard for him to see some of her spark fade.

"How was your party?" he asked, coming around the bed to pick up the photos from her lap.

Confusing.

"It was fun," she said instead.

"And the reason for the trip down memory lane?" he asked, sitting on the side of the bed.

"I was wondering the same thing," Ionie said, opening her eyes.

Their gazes went to her as she softly smiled. "All closed eyes ain't sleep," she said. "Besides, who could rest with all this company in my bedroom?"

"I didn't mean to keep you awake," Jillian said, reaching to hold her hand.

"I was just enjoying you being near me, like when you would spend the weekend with your granddaddy and me," Ionie said, her eyes twinkling with the moonlight streaming into the room. "We would wake up and find you sleep at the foot of the bed, on the bench, or on that cold floor. Like you couldn't stand not being near us. I loved it then and I love it now, Jillie."

That all was so true.

"Mama, you need anything?" Harry asked.

"For Jillie to tell us what's on her mind."

Jillian thought about admitting to her father that she'd had a no-strings-attached relationship and then ended it by accepting her executive chef position.

Hard pass.

"I was dating someone and we ended things," she said, skirting the full truth. "I saw him tonight—"

"At the gala?" her father asked as he scratched his full silver-flecked beard.

She nodded. "Seeing him again made me feel like I care for him more than I realized," she said.

"Do you love him?" Ionie asked, patting Jillian's hand with her own.

Jillian closed her eyes and bit down on her bottom lip as emotion swelled in her chest for Cole. "Yes," she admitted in a whisper.

"Does he love you?" Harry asked with the protectiveness of a father.

She shook her head, remembering Cole's anger with her that night. *And tonight.*

"What?" Harry snapped, rising.

"I broke things off," she said to ease his annoyance.

"Can you fix it?" Ionie asked.

Jillian looked out the window. "I don't want to. I'm not looking for love. Look where it got me before. *Twice,*" she said, her voice soft. "I've always wanted what you and Mom had, Dad. That love story you can tell your kids about thirty years later. But it's just not in the cards for me."

"Life is like a library," Harry said. "It contains so many books because there are many different stories to be told. Each one unique. And special. And needed. Your story may not look like ours, Jillian. Create your own."

She gave her father a teasing smile. "Oh, *Bear,*" she said, ribbing him with her mother's loving nickname.

Ionie chuckled. "Leave my son alone," she playfully

admonished. "Because before he was Bear, he was my Sugar Toes."

Harry gave them both a withering look.

"Sugar Toes," Jillian teased. "Oh *my*."

"I'm going where I'm appreciated," he said over his shoulder as he left the room.

"Might as well, because what she got for you, your Mama and daughter sure can't give you," Ionie called out.

Jillian chuckled as she leaned over to press a kiss to her grandmother's soft cheek. "I love you, Gram," she sighed, lowering her head to rest against her arm.

Ionie reached over with her free hand and rubbed Jillian's loose curls. She hummed them both to sleep with Jillian's heart and thoughts filled with Cole.

"Leave the bustier on."

At Cole's command, Jillian stood before him and unbuttoned her pants before letting the material fall to her feet in a satin puddle. She arched one of her brows and slowly slid her fingers under the rim of her lace panties with the skill of a burlesque dancer. She used tiny rolls of her hips to ease the flimsy lace down around her hips and buttocks.

Cole sat on the bench, leaning back against the foot of the bed as he watched her by the light of the fireplace. She tempted and tantalized him with her slow, sensual movements as they locked eyes. His inches hardened, and stood erect as he ached for her.

Still in her heels, she twirled the flimsy lace on her finger before looping the panties around the tip of his

hardness. She smiled and moved forward to stand be-
tween his open legs then playfully took a bow that low-
ered her head near his lap. With her teeth, she nipped
her panties and removed them to drop to the floor, leav-
ing the tip of his inches free to be covered with her lips.

Cole arched his hips off the bench at the feel of her
tongue tasting him intimately. "Jillian," he gasped as
he pressed his hands to her cheeks and raised her head,
afraid he would burst. He wrapped an arm around her
waist and drew her forward to sit on his lap. He kissed
her deeply, his tongue slowly thrusting in her mouth the
same way he wished he could stand his inches doing so.

"Give it to me, Cole," she pleaded against his mouth,
taking his hardness into her hand to grasp and stroke.

"It's yours," he told her.

Jillian rose from his lap to lower her core onto him
as she gripped the back of his head and licked at his
mouth.

"All mine?" she asked, gripping him with her walls.

With one hard upward thrust, he planted all of him-
self inside her—

Cole awakened from his dream with a start. "Damn,"
he swore, sitting upright and looking down at his erection.

Bzzzzzz. Bzzzzzz. Bzzzzzz.

Another dream about Jillian.

Bzzzzzz. Bzzzzzz. Bzzzzzz.

He swore, ignoring his cell phone vibrating on the
nightstand with calls from his family. It had awakened

him. And now his waking thoughts were filled with Jillian.

That damn bustier of hers is torturing me.

With deep breaths and a wildly pounding heart, he looked around at his hotel suite. And then at his erection. With a grimace, he grabbed a pillow and pressed it against his hardness as he fell back on the bed, unsure if he was more frustrated at still wanting Jillian or at the interruption of his erotic dream of her.

Five

Two weeks later

Jillian used the handle of the pan to rotate it atop the fiery gas range. She grabbed the tall, slender glass of extra-virgin olive oil with her free hand to add it to the root vegetables she was sautéing. Quickly she set it down and grabbed a large pinch of pink salt to sprinkle across the baby carrots, sliced parsnips, leeks and matchstick-sliced rutabagas.

"Three-root-vegetable soup ready, chef," her sous chef called over to her.

She nodded as she turned and used tongs to divide the veggies atop three bowls of puréed soup carefully layered with the flavors of garlic, onion, chicken broth, butter and turmeric. "Run the dish," she ordered, wiping her hands with the dishtowel tucked into the pocket of her monogrammed chef's coat.

"Yes, chef!"

She turned back to the stove and wasn't sure who had obeyed her order as she'd turned it off. Their night at CRESS III was over. Now it was about cleanup and minor prep for the next evening. She allowed herself a smile and a deep exhale of breath, more than ready for a glass of red wine as she sat on her balcony and enjoyed the view.

And try not to think about Cole.

Better said than done.

Against the odds, she had fallen in love over her year of lascivious encounters with Cole. She hadn't planned it. Hadn't even fathomed it possible. She had been wrong. With each passing day now, she *knew* she loved him, but equally knew that she would keep her distance and allow the love to fade with time.

Between his anger at her and her reluctance for a serious relationship, loving him was futile.

And so very foolish.

"Chef, may I have a word with you?"

Jillian stiffened at the sound of Clark Newsom's voice behind her. She turned. His tone was filled with the same arrogance as the tilt of his chin and the slight lift of his left eyebrow.

"Sure," she said, aware of the furtive looks of her staff.

With a stiff smile, she followed the short and slender man in his three-piece suit to his office at the rear of the restaurant. She allowed herself a playful moment as she wrinkled her nose at him. "What's this about, Clark?" she asked the restaurant's manager once she entered the office and he'd closed the door to move past her to take a seat behind his desk.

The menu.

"The menu," he said, echoing her thought.

Jillian slid her hands into the pockets of her coat as she eyed him. "It was a special request, Clark," she said, already knowing that when a patron gave her carte blanche for the side dish with their chicken, she prepared her Lyonnaise potatoes—something not on the menu.

He looked grim and released a long drawn-out breath.

"I am the executive chef, Clark—"

"Of your first restaurant that is part of an international brand," he said, cutting her off.

Jillian fought the urge to rotate her head to release the sudden tension. "When will the training wheels come off, Clark?" she asked, keeping annoyance from her tone.

He stroked his chin. "When you prove you will not let what happened to your first restaurant happen to this one," he said.

Jillian stared at him. Hard. Unrelenting. Cold. Even as the heat of embarrassment warmed her belly. "Until you step from under the protection of the Cress brand and attempt to build something on your own—to fly without a net and risk it all—then don't you dare sit there in your feigned glory and fool yourself into thinking you can look down your nose at me."

"And yet here we both are with that Cress safety net," he countered with a smug look.

Jillian gave him a withering glare before she turned to leave his office, slamming the door behind her. She paused on the other side, hating that he was right. She felt constrained by the reins Cress, INC. had on her culinary creativity. Being watched and scolded. Judged and found lacking to some degree.

But here I am.

She closed her eyes and pinched the bridge of her nose.

And I chose it over Cole.

Her regret was visceral.

Jillian pressed a hand to her belly as she made her way back to the kitchen.

The next morning, Cole drove his all-black vintage Harley-Davidson motorcycle through the streets of Manhattan, enjoying the feel of the wind as he dipped in and out of traffic. Outside of cooking, he felt the freest on the back of his bike.

He slowed to a stop at a red light, sitting between a Land Rover to his left and a white convertible to his right. At the soft beep of a horn, he turned his head to the right to look through the tinted visor of his helmet at a beautiful caramel beauty with freckles and shocking red hair. She slanted him an admiring smile. He raised the visor to reveal his face.

Her smiled widened.

He gave her an appreciative look just as the light turned green, and she pulled off with a wink and wave.

He chuckled before he lowered his visor and accelerated forward as well, guiding his bike between vehicles to leave her behind eventually.

By the time he reached the underground parking garage of the Midtown Manhattan building housing the Cress, INC. offices, he had forgotten the red-headed beauty. The moment of flirtation had been nice, but his focus was not on the sweet intimacies of a woman. Parking his Harley in his assigned spot, he locked it and made his way across the spacious, filled garage in his jeans, boots and a long-sleeved black button-down shirt of crisp cotton. Unlike his brothers, Cole shunned office attire—partly to annoy his father and partly because he found suits constraining and only wore them when necessary.

He rode the elevator up to the fortieth floor. Cress, INC.'s corporate offices occupied the entire floor of the towering building housing offices, a test kitchen, cafeteria, conference room and private dining room for the family. On days his mother wasn't at her renowned culinary school and worked from these offices; she prepared lunch for the family and staff. He stepped off the elevator and crossed the polished floor, pausing as the frosted automatic doors slid open.

Bzzzzzz. Bzzzzzz. Bzzzzzz.

He pulled his phone from the back pocket of his pants.

"Good morning, Mr. Cress," someone said.

"Morning," he said, raising his hand in greeting at the passerby as he looked down at his phone.

His mother was calling.

Their Cold War had to cease—he knew that. Especially with him returning to work.

"Hello," he said.

"Welcome back, son," Nicolette said.

Someone had alerted her to his presence. The concept of Big Brother had nothing on a curious mother—especially a powerhouse like Nicolette Lavoie-Cress.

"How can I help you, Mama?" he asked, aware that his tone was still cool and distant with her as he made his way down the wide hall to his office. He gave his brothers Luc and Sean a wave through the glass wall of their offices.

"The family is doing an interview and cover shoot for *Scrumptious*," she said of Cress, INC.'s flagship magazine.

He entered his office, pausing to take in the sight of the Manhattan skyline outside the floor-to-ceiling windows. The sun was bright and its rays almost blinded him.

Jillian had loved the feel of the sun on her naked body. He remembered mornings she would lie on a yoga mat beneath the loft windows to relish the beams as they warmed her body, giving it a golden glow. Never had he seen anything more beautiful.

"Cole?"

"I can't make it," he said, jarred from his memory. "You know I run my food truck on the weekends."

The chair behind his deck swiveled to the front, revealing his mother sitting in it.

"Rather dramatic. Don't you think?" Cole asked as

he walked over to his ebony desk and set his phone facedown upon it along with his keys.

Nicolette stood, looking beautiful in a tailored black-silk pantsuit. "Not unlike you disappearing," she said before opening her arms wide and bending her fingers to beckon him. "I haven't hugged my son in months. Let's fix that ASAP, Cole."

He stepped into her embrace, towering over her height.

Nicolette rose on her toes in her heels. "I did things wrong, but I meant well," she said. "Forgive me?"

Cole stepped back and busied himself pushing his shirtsleeves up his arms before claiming his seat. "Forgive? Yes. Forget? Not yet," he said.

"Even if my actions revealed the flaw of blind ambition in Jillian?" she asked.

He stiffened as he stared at his mother hard. "You and I will never discuss Jillian Rossi," he said.

Nicolette held up her hands as if conceding. "We need you at the interview," she said, switching gears.

"I'm available at any time outside of the weekend," he said, logging on to his computer.

"Your food truck wasn't important to you during your…sabbatical," his mother pointed out as she walked around to claim one of the seats in front of his desk.

"So, you could imagine my urgency to get back to it as soon as possible," he countered.

Nicolette eased her hands into the pockets of her pants. "When you were a toddler, you clung to me more than any of your brothers—even Lucas once he was born," she said.

Cole steeled himself. She was going into full guilt mode and pulling at heartstrings. His mother was the best at it.

"You would love for me to pull you in my lap and read to you," she continued with twinkling blue eyes and a genuine smile. "It was the best. Just me and my little Cole Man. The sound of your little raspy voice asking me to read some more was better than a flawlessly cooked soufflé. Just perfection."

She sighed.

"What went wrong, Cole?" she asked. *"Pourquoi me deetestes-tu?"*

He chuckled and tapped his fingers atop his desk as he eyed her. "I don't hate you," he answered her question. "I was angry at you for interfering in my life, and I need to make it clear to you not to do it again. It feels disrespectful as a grown man."

She nodded in understanding. "It is not easy to accept that your boys—"

"Sons," he interjected.

"Fine, Cole," she snapped before releasing a long breath as she balled her hand into a fist and pressed the side of it to her mouth. "You're grown."

"Thirty," he stressed. "Your youngest is twenty-nine."

"Don't remind me," she muttered.

Cole chuckled again.

Nicolette eyed him and then offered the smile that made America love her. "Cole, this weekend is the only time available for *Scrumptious'* team to get in and get it all done to make the deadline for the mag to go to print."

He remained quiet.

She nodded, taking his silence for consent. "Thank you," she said with emphasis as she stroked her hair, which was fast becoming more silver than blond.

He gave her a brief nod before turning his attention to his emails. His team's most recent analytics report showed a plateau or steady decline across all online social media platforms and the massive company website.

"I'll be meeting with my team today regarding a redesign and relaunch of the website," he said as he opened the site and frowned at its slowness to upload.

"I know you have no real interest in the CEO position—"

"At *all*," he insisted.

"My rebel," she said softly.

He glanced over at her. She was his mother and he adored her—flaws and all. So he offered her his smile.

"Knowing you don't want it, I'm proud of you for still taking the initiative, and I look forward to hearing more about your plans," Nicolette said.

In truth, he was looking for a diversion from his thoughts now that he was away from the intoxicating recreation of Europe. The project would help him focus on something else besides...

Missing Jillian.

Nicolette rose from her seat to walk across to the office's glass entryway. She paused beside his name etched in the glass. "Will you be home tonight, *mon fils*?" she asked of her son without turning around.

Cole frowned. He didn't enjoy hurting his mother. He had simply just respected the anger she'd caused in him and allowed himself time to forgive and move on. So he knew his next words would be a blow. "I have a real-estate agent looking for condos…" he began, opening and closing his hand into a fist that he was sure must feel like the grip on her heart. That comparison led him to press his palm flat against the desktop. "Until then, I'll be staying with Gabe and Monica."

She stiffened.

Her love for her children was not in question. Never.

"I need privacy. I'm a grown man, but maybe it's hard to respect that if I'm still living under the same roof as the entire family at thirty," Cole explained.

Saying no more, Nicolette left his office and walked away. The sound of her heels against the polished tiled floor soon faded.

Cole wiped his hand over his mouth, longing for the days when his life was much simpler. When annoying his father was the most demanding task of his day. Adoring his mother without question. Felt the loyal bond between him and his brothers. Enjoyed the time spent cooking in his beloved food truck. And finding the sweetest no-ties, uncomplicated passion with Jillian.

Now?

Everything seemed disjointed. He felt shattered into pieces and twisting in the wind.

He hated it.

One week later

"You look amazing, Jillian."

She gave her date a warm look as they danced to the

jazz band in the club that had recreated the vintage feel of Harlem. "Thank you," she said, offering him a smile that belied the nervousness she felt.

Miles Fairmount was the handsome, well-built man who owned the market where they purchased live seafood for CRESS III. After several offers for dinners, Jillian had finally accepted—desperately in search of a remedy for the "I love Cole Cress" blues. She needed all the help she could get.

Seeking a connection, Jillian raised her hand from his shoulder to his nape and leaned a bit closer to lightly rest her forehead against his chest. She inhaled his cologne and closed her eyes as they swayed to the music.

But all she could think of was that Miles wasn't as tall as Cole, who could easily rest his chin atop her head and whose height forced her to lean back to look up into his face. And his cologne was spicier than the cool notes Cole preferred. Because of Miles's bald head, there were no soft curls to tease on his neck. His hand on her back felt unfamiliar. They were not moving in sync.

He was not Cole.

Jillian released a heavy sigh.

Miles paused. "Everything okay?" he asked.

Her eyes studied his face. He was a handsome man. A nice man. Successful and charming.

But not Cole.

That blue-eyed playboy has me all messed up.

Miles chuckled and raised her arm above her head to slowly spin her before gently guiding her body back against his. "I don't have a chance. Do I?" he asked, sounding amused.

He's insightful.

Jillian offered him an apologetic look. "You would—"

"If…" he offered.

She nodded and bit the corner of her bottom lip.

"So where is he?" Miles asked as he danced them in a circle among the other dancers on the black floor with its red-hued lighting that harmonized the soulful ambience.

"Not with me," she admitted in his ear, feeling the loss of Cole as tangible as the pain of a deep cut.

"Is he on his way back?" Miles gently maneuvered her into a dip and then lightly jerked her body back up against his.

Okay, this is fun, Jillian admitted to herself.

"No," she admitted to him.

"Then maybe you should go to him," Miles offered before he raised her arm for another twirl.

And say what?

Forgive me? Understand me? Have me?

I love you?

But did she want a relationship with Cole or anyone else? Did she want to put her heart out there just to be disappointed? Was Cole worth risking it all?

I'm already heartbroken.

And her biggest fear pulsed with a life all its own deep inside her, causing sleepless nights and nail-biting sessions.

Just because I love him doesn't mean he loves me.

As Miles twirled them around the crowded floor, her thoughts filled with Cole's anger. Their fling had lasted longer than expected. Why was he so angry at her? That she'd chosen her career over great sex? Or...

"Miles?" Jillian said. "Can I get a male point of view on something? Is that okay? It's about *him*."

"Sure."

Although she felt uncomfortable talking to her date about another man, she longed for a male perspective on something that had nagged at her of late. "What would cause a man to be so angry about a woman ending a no-strings attachment?" she asked.

He continued to sway as he considered her question. "Depends..." he began. "Could be I'm an egomaniac refusing to admit a woman would want to end things and feeling I should have been the one to do it."

That made her wince slightly.

"*Or...* I cared for her more than even I knew I did," he offered.

Hope sprung to life in her chest.

"*Or...* I felt betrayed," he finished.

Her gut clenched. At that moment, Miles had hit the nail on the head of her assessment and could be called MC Hammer.

"So, if she chose a great job in San Fran offered to her by one of his loved ones to ensure the end of their relationship?" she asked near his ear, her voice tentative.

Miles leaned back to look at her. "He may think you used him for a come-up," he suggested.

"Right. I didn't, but I can see how he may think that," Jillian admitted, feeling so weary that she allowed her head to rest against his shoulder.

Miles chuckled and patted her back consolingly.

Jillian you're on a date!

She jerked up her head. "I'm sorry," she said, regaining her composure.

"In the words of Usher, you got it bad," he said. "The only thing to do is a have conversation...*with him*."

It was her time to chuckle. "Am I the worst date ever?" she asked.

He spun her away and then pulled her back to him. "Sadly, not at all," he said dryly.

That drew a full laugh from her—head flung back and all.

"For tonight, let's enjoy some good fun and good music," Miles said. "And when I see you Tuesday at the market, we'll just share a friendly smile and remember we wished each other well in our love lives...apart."

"Deal," Jillian agreed.

Miles took several steps back as he swayed their hands between them. *Dance*, he mouthed.

She did, holding the flared skirt of her red dress as she gently rocked her hips. It felt good to focus on the music and not work, missing her family or Cole—for at least a little while.

Cole released a yawn and set his laptop beside him on the bed as he sat back against the tall leather headboard. He checked his watch. It was well after midnight. He had been going through mockups for the new web design and overseeing plans for a massive launch party. He'd been at it all day and long after arriving at Gabe and Monica's sprawling Tribeca condo.

Wearing navy pajamas that were totally for the sake

of modesty while living with his brother and his fian-cée, Cole left the bed and crossed the large room to use both hands to open the French doors. The heat of summer was fading quickly as early fall was approaching. He looked down at the street from the towering height, taking in the traffic, the bright lights and the still fast pace of New Yorkers even with the late hour.

There was a time when he would have been among them, searching for fast times and faster women to while away the late hours. Over the last year, Jillian's apartment had appealed to him more. Just being there with her—laughing, cooking, watching silly television shows, or lost in the heat of their desire for each other—had satisfied him. That year had led to him no longer seeking—or needing—the nightlife.

But, just as he'd feared, being back among the New York streets was a poignant reminder of Jillian. He ached for her and then felt anger at being so foolish to do so.

She made her choice.

He closed his eyes and grated his teeth. It *still* bothered him.

He hadn't been ready for their time to end, and it didn't sit well that she had. It felt so disloyal to him. So underhanded.

Even though they had always maintained a no-strings attachment.

Even though neither had talked about forever.

He hadn't even thought about it like that before.

That made him frown at his conflicted feelings. Was

it that he'd wanted to be the one to end it? Was it all about his ego?

Cole thought about that. Searching within himself for his truth. In the end, he shook his head.

His lingering doubt: had getting an executive chef position at a Cress restaurant been Jillian's real motivation to work as their private chef or to get involved with him.

Did she use me?

His anger resurfaced.

Balling and releasing his hand at the tension in his body that fought for release, Cole reentered the guest bedroom. He crossed the hardwood floor with bare feet to leave the suite and walk down the darkened hallway to the kitchen in search of a late-night snack.

"Deeper, Gabe. Go deeper."

Cole froze at Monica's words echoing in the hall.

The door to the master suite was slightly ajar, and it was clear Gabe and Monica were having a late-night snack of their own. His stomach grumbled, but he didn't dare walk past their door. Turning, he returned to his suite and closed the door securely behind him, resigning himself to sleep off his hunger.

Long after settling beneath the covers in the cloak of darkness, he realized it was not just food for which he yearned. His brother had found love; they shared their lives. Loving each other. Taking care of one another. Making love to each other.

As he lay in his bed with nothing but his anger at Jillian to clutch, he felt alone and hungry for a partner of his own. That was a discovery he hadn't been aware of or ready to accept. For so long, he had rebelled against what was expected and ordinary. He had found comfort in being different.

As he buried his head against the pillow, the rebel was willing to admit that he had been wrong.

Six

One week later

"Jillian. Jillian? Something wrong?"

She heard the voice beside her as she stood there, but she was unable to speak. For her, time, and everything along with it, slowed as she looked across the distance with no doubt. Her body was sure of him, even when her eyes were not. Shock, pleasure, and fighting the urge to run to him with the fancy of a child left her spellbound.

Cole, she mouthed as she watched him work from his large navy-colored food truck that was a showpiece all its own.

As he handed someone their order, he raised his head as if he had heard her call his name—but that was impossible because it had been less than a whisper. His eyes widened at the sight of her. He was just as surprised as she was.

Did he also feel the pull to eat up the distance between them? The urge to be near her?

It nearly suffocated her.

"You okay, Jillian?"

"Yes," she lied to her former first husband, hating the hand Warren placed at the small of her back as he stood beside her.

Cole's expression changed. Hardened as he'd turned his head and focused on taking an order from the next person in a very long line of customers waiting to purchase his food.

"I'm glad we met up, Jillie," Warren said, using her childhood nickname.

He would know it well. They had been high school sweethearts who had married right after graduation and then divorced a year later when marriage, college and finances had not mixed.

She looked up at him with a genuine smile. "Me, too, Dr. Long."

When she'd been told that significant renovation would close the restaurant for two weeks, she had been more than happy to post on social media that she was headed home to the east coast. Warren had reached out to let her know that he had moved back from Texas. That he'd taken an esteemed position as an attending cardiothoracic surgeon in Manhattan.

A day enjoying good music and a bevy of good eats at a food truck rally in Prospect Park in Brooklyn had seemed the ideal place for a friendly reconnection.

They'd spoken here and there over the years, often via social media, but both had long since released ideas of reconciliation and were just happy for friendship and nothing more.

"The only thing missing to make me feel like I'm home truly is *pizza*," she stressed, ignoring the nervousness she felt at just what Cole thought of her being there with another man.

"It would be bagels for me," Warren said, easing his black-framed glasses up on his nose as he looked around. "There're still a good number of trucks on this side. I wish I wasn't on duty tonight."

"It's cool," she said, shifting her eyes to Cole's truck. He had the most massive crowd awaiting a chance to order from the well-known celebrity cook. "I know that chef, and I'm gonna jump on board to help."

"Really?" he asked. "Cool. You have a way home?"

"Warren, I'm a grown woman, not the high school girl you first met," she reminded him.

"And you've survived a long time without me around," he said, sounding bemused.

"Same for you. I am so proud of you, Warren."

"And you're an executive chef," he said, looking down at his feet and then up at her. "We both are living our dreams."

"I think getting out of our nightmare of a marriage played a *huge* role," she said.

"I agree." Warren chuckled.

Following an impulse, Jillian reached up to pat his chest as she felt the twinkle in her eyes. "Go save lives, and I'll go cook," she said, feeling comfortable around him.

Warren gave her another smile before turning to stride away.

Jillian licked her lips as she walked over to Cole's truck. The smell of food mingled in the air with the music played on the main stage. She didn't know if she was crazy or not, but she followed her instincts and the road that led back to Cole. Her heart guided her.

"Excuse me," she said, easing between two women in line to climb the steps and open the door to the polished food truck. "Need some help?"

Cole did a double-take—maybe even a triple—as he paused with a handful of sliced green onions above an open takeout container. He knit his brows as he finished the dish and handed it to his customer with a smile.

It had been so long since he'd beamed that disarming tool at her.

"One moment," he said to the next person in line.

Jillian's heart hammered as she closed the metal door and reached for one of the black aprons hanging from a hook.

He walked over to her. "Get out, Jillian," he said coldly. "I don't want you here."

Her ego caused her spine to stiffen and she had to give herself a quick five count. *Fight for him. Don't give up.* "But you need me," she told him, shifting to his left to try to pass.

Cole moved to block her.

She looked up and their eyes locked. She released a little puff of breath to relieve the electricity she felt at being so close to him. Inhaling his scent. Getting lost in his eyes. Wanting to feel his touch.

She craved Cole Cress. It was a profound hunger fueled by love. She had to bite her lip to keep from revealing her heart to him. "You want to waste time arguing with me while your patrons wait, *Chef*?" she asked.

He turned and moved away from her with strides that revealed his annoyance. "You sure you're *allowed* to help me?" he asked as he grabbed a towel and looked down at his hands as he wiped them.

"Allowed by whom?" she asked, stepping to the small sink to wash her hands before quickly surveying the ingredients in his fridge and the items offered on the menu.

The food truck was far more than that. It was a compact chef's kitchen with all the bells and whistles. She felt excited to play with his beloved toy.

"My mother…and *your* man," Cole grumbled.

He's jealous.

"Your mother does not own me, and the gentleman you saw me with was my ex-husband, not my current man," she said, shifting to stand beside him and smile down at a young woman. "What can I get for you?"

At that point, they were off to the races and spent the next few hours splitting the grill to make the orders and trim the order line down. Long after darkness descended and the towering light poles of the park had to bring illumination, the two worked in sync, even helping each other with a particular order and using a shorthand to get the job done, fast, efficiently and, most important, deliciously.

Jillian found it exhilarating.

The close quarters and having to brush past Cole had stoked her desire. At times, she would notice the muscles of his arms as he reached to hand a customer their plate, or the way he used a cloth to dab at the sweat dampening his forehead, or the scent of his cologne mingling with the onion and spices in the air. The fit of his jeans on his buttocks. The small of his back when he reached for something from the shelf above his head.

The smile he offered each and every person.

A charmer. *Her* charmer.

Or at least, he would be again.

She bit the inside of her cheek as she envisioned licking away the sweat dampening his chest. The impulse to be near him and to reconnect with him had been too tempting to deny. The very sight of him flooded her body with that undeniable warmth of love.

Jillian decided that she wanted Cole back in her life, no matter the consequences.

"All right. Thank you. 'Night," he said to his last customer before sliding the window closed and pressing a button to automatically lower the awning.

"All the bells and whistles," she said as she finished wiping and sanitizing the stainless-steel countertops. "This is top of the line, Cole."

He nodded as he removed his apron. "I only like the best of the best," he said.

"Oh. Well…thank you," Jillian said with a flirty curtsy.

Cole eyed her for so long with a blank expression that she felt foolish.

She threw her hands up in frustration.

"I was referring to things that are mine," he said.

"I'm not a *thing*," she shot back.

"Nor were you mine," he returned coldly in retaliation.

"I don't *belong* to anyone," she stated, stressing the word.

Cole smirked and dropped his head as he shook it.

"You treat me like we never shared a year—"

"Are you serious?" He balked with wide-eyed astonishment. "And you treated me any better? Don't be a hypocrite, Jillian. You chose your career over me—and didn't give me the respect to talk to me about it first."

"A big scene wasn't part of the deal. Be fair," Jillian said. "We were never meant to be serious."

Cole took a step closer to her. "What was part of it?" he asked.

Jillian leaned back against the counter as she looked up into his eyes. "What?"

"It. Us. Whatever we were," he said, his eyes dipping down to her mouth.

She licked at it with the tip of her tongue. "It was just sex. Great sex," she whispered into the heat rising between them. "No strings. Remember?"

"Oh. I remember. I wish I could forget," Cole said, looking tortured as he gripped her waist and easily lifted her to sit atop the counter.

She spread her legs and reached to press her hands against his shoulders before gripping his T-shirt. "Cole," she gasped in that hot little moment before he dipped his head to kiss her mouth.

The first feel of his lips was electrifying. She shivered and clung to him with the jolt as they pressed their upper bodies together and deepened the kiss with a moan that burst with their hunger for one another. With each passing second, their movements rushed—almost wild and desperate as they undressed each other. Unbuttoning. Unzipping. Pulling up, over. Yanking down. Until they were nude. And panting between kisses.

He put hands on either side of her atop the counter as he looked at her with heated eyes. She rubbed his sides with her knees as she leaned in to lick at his lips. He caught her tongue and sucked it deeply into his mouth before releasing it to press kisses to her neck and the deep valley between her breasts.

"Cole," she moaned in sweet agony, flinging her head back.

Each lick of his tongue against a taut brown nipple made her shiver and cry out.

Each deep suckle led to her arching her back as if to offer him more to taste. To enjoy. To have.

She reached between them to grip his inches—gasping at the heat and the hardness.

He hissed in pleasure as she stroked him. With a grunt, he rolled his hips, thrusting his tool against her palm as he wildly licked at her breasts. "Jillian... Jillian... Jillian," he moaned.

"Now, Cole," she gasped, needing him to ease the throbbing ache of desire. "Now."

He honored her demand and used his narrow hips to guide his smooth tip into her swiftly with one deep thrust.

She cried out and arched her back at the feel of him. The hardness. The heat. The perfect snug fit. The strokes. She ached and pulsed in places she had ignored as she had longed for only his touch and denied seeking pleasure with anyone else. And in the heat, it all was so achingly familiar. She leaned into it. Accepting the unique connection they shared—setting aside doubts and any promises or deals made to claim her desire for this man. Along with her passion, her heart swelled with emotion for him as she felt the wave of her climax rise.

No longer could she deny the truth to herself or to him. "I love you, Cole," she whimpered as she gasped with each of his deep, long, and strong strokes. "I love you *so* much."

Cole stiffened and stopped midstroke. Sweat dripped from his body onto hers as he stared at her.

Still releasing deep breaths with his hardness deep inside her as she clutched and released him with her walls, she looked up. Her eyes searched his as she waited for the next words that would come out of his beautiful mouth.

"Don't do that, Jillian," Cole said, his voice stern. *Damn.*

There was no more glorious sight to Cole than Jillian naked, her eyes glazed, mouth panting, and breasts pointed high, his hardness buried deep within her. But she'd ruined it with her declaration of love. The very last thing he wanted was to be toyed with or placated.

When he'd first spotted Jillian with another man, his undeniable jealousy had rushed at him. It had conquered any other emotion and distracted him from his work. Thoughts of another man enjoying her sexuality had plagued him.

"Do what?" she asked as she continued to use the inner walls of her intimacy to clutch and release his inches.

"Use the love card," he countered with a quickness. "You didn't love me. Love would've led to you choosing me and not a job."

"I do love you. I didn't realize it until I'd lost you—"

"Tossed me aside," he countered.

"Cole, I didn't know," she said, sitting upright to press kisses to his chin and mouth. "I thought we could just walk away from each other and it would mean nothing, but it does. I can't stop thinking of you and missing you and wanting you. I dream of you inside me. Deeply. So deep. Just like now."

Her words, kisses and touches were irrefutable. His body was caught in her trap and he didn't want to escape. Her tongue dipped inside his mouth and touched his. That caused him to shiver. She began to work her hips back and forth, sending her sliding on his inches. He got harder.

"Jillian," he moaned into her mouth as he gripped her hips.

She pressed her lush breasts against his chest and wrapped her arms around his neck. "Did you miss me, Cole?" she asked, looking into his eyes.

He refused to answer even as he enjoyed the feel of her core easing back and forth on him.

Jillian kissed a trail to his ear and sucked the lobe. "Do you forgive me, Cole?" she whispered.

He shivered but bit down on his bottom lip to keep quiet.

"Don't you want me back, Cole?" she asked as she eased her core to his throbbing tip and paused to kiss it with her lips before easing down onto him again.

He flung his head back and released a hoarse cry. She knew all too well how sensitive his tip was.

Jillian smiled as she drew her knees up to her shoulders, causing her walls to tighten along on his hardness.

He drew his lips into a circle and gave her a long stare he knew was intense. "Jillian…" he warned.

"Oh, so you *can* talk," she said lightly before circling her hips clockwise and then counterclockwise.

Just the sight of the snakelike movement of her hips was an enticing as the feel of her. He winced as he pressed his hands to his face. No one knew his body, and how to arouse him, like Jillian. But, in turn, *he* knew her just as well. And he felt like being a little more in control.

He had to, or Jillian would know the truth that he could no longer deny.

The root of his anger was the aching of his heart.

He lowered his hands to her hips to stop the hypnotic, rhythmic motion.

Jillian leaned back to look at him.

Their eyes searched each other's faces.

Cole lowered his lids slightly as the look in her eyes

shifted from desire to something more profound. More vulnerable. More revealing. Raw. Real.

His heart skipped a beat and he felt his feelings for her tighten his chest. The battle whether to trust her or not raged within him. "What more do you want from me? From my family?" he asked, his voice as hard as the inches still buried inside her.

Her eyes filled with remorse and glistened with unshed tears. "Let me love you," she whispered on a breath before closing her eyes and shaking her head with her regret.

Damn.

Her pain caused the same in him. It pierced.

Jillian opened her eyes, her lashes damp with tears she'd held in, and looked at him. She gasped and covered her mouth with her hand. "You really care about me, too, Cole," she said.

He shut his eyes.

She pressed her hands to his face and kissed his mouth. Gently. Lovingly.

"Don't you have a deal to keep with my mother?" he said. He tilted his head back to avoid her tempting kisses and to attempt to hold steadfast to anger that was fading.

"I choose you," she said.

"Too late," he said.

"Cole," she said, revealing a streak of frustration with him.

He surprised himself by the urge to chuckle and was relieved when he didn't.

Again, she started to rotate her hips. He was unable to deny that he missed her in his bed, but he also yearned for the sound of her laughter and her free-spirited nature in his life. "I don't believe you are in love with me," he admitted as he shifted his hands to grip her buttocks.

Jillian lowered one arm across his back and settled the other on his shoulder as she kissed one side of his mouth and then the other.

"I will prove it to you, Cole Cress," she whispered against his lips.

He lightly gripped the back of her neck and kissed her deeply, wanting to eat her words. She moaned from the back of her throat as he sucked her tongue and delivered a thrust that eased the rest of his inches inside her until she was full with him.

They moved in sync in a wicked back-and-forth motion. Desire and passion fueled them. Moans and pants and hot, whispered words of praise and pleading filled the air as they gave in to the attraction that had pulsed between them from the first sight of one another.

The months of denying himself the treats of another woman now had him feeling quite wild. He had to fight not to give in to it and perhaps thrust too hard or deep. The urge to leave love marks upon her neck and breasts filled him, but again he resisted the temptation to suckle and bite her flesh. He felt excitement and pleasure. His body began to seek and crave his release, but he eyed her intently as he honed in on a change in her intimacy that hinted she, too, was near climax.

He took the lead, delivering deep, slow strokes that made her eyes seem to glaze as she bit her bottom lip.

He raised one of her legs over his arm and shifted a bit to the left to match his thrusts with his racing heartbeat. Fast and furious. Her eyes widened and her mouth gaped as she dug her fingernails into his buttocks. He grunted and hissed as he felt her walls grip and release him.

She was primed and ready.

And so was he.

"You want it?" Cole asked, his voice deep and intense.

"Please," she begged in a hot little whisper in his ear.

He shivered as he shifted her leg he held on to his shoulder and turned his head to kiss her calf as he let loose a series of piston-like strokes to stoke the storm bursting to explode.

Jillian turned his face and licked at his lips. "Yes," she gasped against his mouth before she winced and cried out as her body shook with her release.

He met her on the apex, licking at her mouth before releasing a roar to match that of a lion as he got lost in white-hot spasms and euphoria.

They both breathed into one another's open mouth and stared in each other's eyes. When he stopped his thrusts, she took the lead in their explosive ride, wanting to push him right over the edge into madness. His rough cry was her reward as Jillian used her legs around his waist to keep him from running from her skill. She didn't stop until all of his hardness was eased.

Cole felt relief.

When a tear raced along her cheek as she clung to him, he pressed a comforting kiss to it and then to her neck.

"I do love you, Cole," she whispered beseechingly.

He just couldn't allow himself to embrace that emotion.

Not yet.

Jillian glanced at Cole as they worked in silence to clean and sanitize the food truck. Her cheeks warmed as she wiped down the counter where they had enjoyed each other for the first time in months. She noticed he moved with the same slowness that she did. They were drained. Truly, sleep was the only remedy after exhaustive and mind-altering sex.

He glanced up from sweeping the floor and caught her stare on him.

She locked her eyes with his and felt a surge of energy from his look. They shared a smile—a naughty one.

"You missed me," she said, just slightly teasing.

He chuckled and tapped the push broom against the tiled floor. "I missed you," he admitted.

She dropped the sponge she was using and closed the gap between them to wrap her arm around his waist as she pressed her cheek to his muscular back. "I'll be back soon. I just have to give my notice to the restaurant—"

"No, you don't," he said.

She froze and stepped back as he turned.

"Keep the position," Cole said.

That made her nervous.

"All I ever wanted was a choice in the matter and not to be treated like your personal sex slave," he said.

"And I'm ready to give us a serious try," she said.

"I'm not," he said, continuing to sweep the floor. "Plus, you may change your mind."

Jillian knew she had destroyed whatever trust he'd had in her, and she was determined to prove to him that he could trust in her and, in time, one day love her.

I hope.

"How do you suppose we see each other?" she asked, feeling some of her own fears about love resurfacing.

"If it matters to us, then *we* will make a way," Cole said.

She nodded as she finished ensuring all surfaces were sanitary to prepare food. Still, doubts plagued her.

Should I trust him? Am I wasting my time?

She released a breath.

Why is love so dang on complicated?

Cole came up to stand behind her. "What's on your mind?" he asked. "I can see it on your face."

Nothing.

But that was a lie and wouldn't help her build the same trust for which she yearned.

She leaned back against his strong body, wondering how she'd missed how secure she felt in his presence and how observant he had always been to her moods. "Love wasn't a part of my plan, Cole, but here I am, loving you," she said, speaking her truth as she turned to look up at him. "And it scares me."

In the depths of his grayish-blue eyes, she saw the fear of her own reflected.

Cole wrapped his arms around her and bent his head to press a kiss to her forehead. "I will always be honest with you, Jillian, and that's all I'm asking from you," he promised. "I give you my word that I won't lead you on."

She nodded, enjoying the light massage he was giving her back. She felt her desire rising as his hands slipped under her shirt and pressed to her skin with warmth, but she couldn't run from her doubts and the fact that she already had two marriages under her belt.

The only thing she knew for sure was how much she missed Cole in her life, and having him back was worth the risk.

Because not having him had been torture.

Seven

Two weeks later

Cole's footsteps echoed inside the two-thousand-foot condo in the Chelsea section of Manhattan's west side. It was empty of furniture—save for the king-size bed in the owner's suite. The post-war nineteen-story building's structural design was evident in the modern lines, towering eleven-foot ceilings, polished teak hardwood floors, and views of the Hudson River via the expansive windows.

But it was the neighborhood that had clutched it for him. Chelsea offered a mix of culture, nightlife and art that suited him well. He didn't even mind the traffic noise that reached the ninth floor because it spoke the neighborhood's vibe. Art galleries, restaurants, shopping and gourmet food markets were in abundance among the new and old residential structures.

There was always something to do and to see.

His stomach rumbled in hunger.

"And to eat," he said.

Bzzzzzz. Bzzzzzz. Bzzzzzz.

He pulled his phone from the back pocket of his denims. His smile was not to be denied at a FaceTime call from Jillian. He answered. "Hello, Chef," he said, holding the phone up to his face as he took in hers.

She was beautiful as ever, with her curly hair piled atop her head and her face fresh of any makeup. Her brown eyes twinkled as she gave him a smile that beamed. "How are you, Chef?" she asked, standing on her terrace, the waterfront in the background.

Missing you.

"I know I'm missing you like crazy," she said, seeming to steal his thought. "I hated to leave you yesterday."

"Me, too," he admitted, walking down the long, wide hall to the owner's suite. "It was hard sleeping without you."

"Even in that big beautiful bed?" she asked.

He chuckled. "It felt bigger without you in it," he admitted.

"Then I gotta get back to it real soon."

Good.

For the last two weeks, they had been nearly inseparable and how they'd spent that time together ran the gamut. From long rides across the city on his motorcycle to mind-blowing sexcapades. Long conversations about their careers and their families. Cooking and feeding each other. Sometimes saying nothing and just enjoying the comfort of being together lounging naked in bed as the rain poured outside.

"You made a good choice," he said, eyeing the king-size structure that sat in the middle of his bedroom, the covers strewed everywhere.

"Thank you," she said as the San Francisco winds blew the escaped tendrils back from her face.

His feelings for her had deepened.

Jillian was making it impossible not to do so. She was putting on a full-court press to prove she loved him and wanted him in her life. Never had *he* been wooed with having his favorite meals prepared, surprising him with thoughtful gifts, and continuous declarations of her love as they invested time in each other.

And the sex.

He shook his head at how it had only intensified once deeper feelings had been added to the mix. Nothing felt better than looking down into Jillian's eyes as he stroked deep within her and seeing them flooded with her emotions and, at times, tears of sweet release.

It was addictive.

And he felt himself crave her.

"I just wanted to see that face before I headed to the restaurant," she said, walking back inside her apartment. "I'm excited to see the changes."

"Call me when you're done and tell me about it. I'll be up," Cole said, taking steps to the kitchen that centered the condo. He picked up the stack of takeout menus.

"Something to look forward to," she said as she

leaned the phone against something to pull a lightweight jacket over the fitted long-sleeved tee she wore with her black uniform pants.

His doorbell rang loudly.

"Someone has company," she said, jerking a leather satchel over her head to settle on her side.

"Gabe and Mo wanted to see the place," he told her, walking over to the door.

"Speaking of family…" Jillian picked up the phone and walked down the hall to reach her front door. "My grandmother believes you're beautiful and wants to know if I didn't bring you around because I was scared she would steal you from me."

Cole chuckled, remembering and liking the feisty silver-haired woman with pink-painted lips. Dinner with Jillian's family had been a surprise that he'd enjoyed. Her mother was warm. Her father, a solid man. And her grandmother simply adorable with a quick wit and a flirty eye wink. "Beautiful, huh?" he asked as he stood by the condo's front door.

"Funny, you chose to focus on *that*," she mused.

They laughed.

"Enjoy your visit, and please check with your interior decorator on your *furniture*," she quipped before blowing him a kiss and ending the call.

Cole made a mental note to do that in the morning as he slid his phone into his back pocket and opened the front door. "Do I smell food?" he asked, looking down at the bags they carried.

"Wow. Hello to you, too, Cole," Monica said, rising on her toes to kiss his cheek before walking inside.

Gabe chuckled as he offered his brother his fist for a tap with his own in greeting. "Don't let her fool you. She is starving, too," he said, offering his future bride an amused look when she shot him a playful glare before looking up at the towering tray ceiling.

"This condo is *beautiful*," she said, making a slow turn to take in the abundance of floor-to-ceiling windows that offered a view of the sun descending on the Manhattan skyline.

Cole led Gabe into the kitchen, where he set the bags he carried atop the sizable marble island. "It will be better once Jaime gets it decorated," he said, opening the custom cabinets to remove plates.

The kitchen was stocked with essentials because he and Jillian had enjoyed staying in and cooking for each other.

"Jaime Pine Design?" Monica asked, removing the lightweight emerald-green trench she wore with matching slacks and a light silk sweater. "Good choice."

"I always liked what she did with the townhouse," Cole said as she took Gabe's navy jacket and set both garments atop the empty counter.

"Does Mother know?" Gabe asked, opening the containers of steaming Thai food.

"I didn't tell her," Cole said as he piled a plate high with saucy beef noodles, green papaya salad and *pak boong* sautéed in traditional spicy Thai flavors. Several small omelets made with shrimp and green onions made a food tower he planned to demolish. "The last thing I need is her interfering in my life again."

Gabe and Monica shared a look.

"You ready to talk about just what she did to end things with you and Jillian?" Gabe asked, leaning against the counter and taking a bite from a grilled pork skewer.

"She got between Jillian and me," Cole said, covering his lips with the back of his hand as he spoke with his mouth full—something his mother abhorred.

Monica smiled at him as she opened a bottle of white wine. "Who knew you were a note writer? It's so romantic."

Cole was surprised she knew that.

"I found one in the kitchen and I read it—felt scandalous for doing so—and quickly put it back," she said as she searched and found the cabinet holding wine goblets.

"Where was it?" Cole asked as Gabe looked on at their exchange.

"In her knife case," Monica said, giving him a playful wink before she poured half a glass of wine for each of them.

He bit back a smile and hung his head, remembering that particular note well.

The taste of you still lingers on my tongue.

The night before, he had spent nearly an hour savoring Jillian intimately while bringing her to one explosive climax after another.

"You didn't tell me you found a note," Gabe said to her.

"And you didn't tell me your little brother and the chef were doing the do," Monica countered.

Gabe raised his glass to her.

She touched hers to his.

"Touché," they said in unison.

Cole eyed them, loving their vibe together. Monica had softened his brother, and never had he seen him smile so much. Jillian did the same for him. His rebellious brooding was not as constant.

And his mother had contributed to taking that from him.

"Mom offered Jillian the chef position to end things with me," Cole said, filling the silence and giving in to the sudden need to share his frustration with their mother.

"Damn." Gabe frowned. "Are you sure?"

"She didn't know I was in Jillian's apartment, and I heard it all myself," Cole said.

The frown became a scowl.

"Perhaps it's time I share something." Monica took a deep sip of wine before moving over to wrap an arm around Gabe's waist.

He looked wary.

"She did the same with me." Monica finished dryly, "But *I* didn't get a job offer."

"What!" Gabe roared.

Monica winced as she held him tighter and recounted Nicolette's coming to the charity ball she threw for the nonprofit foundation she'd developed to help young adults aging out of the foster care system. "She warned me that our relationship would never survive. But she was wrong."

"You never told me that," Gabe said, looking down at her upturned face.

Cole shook his head at the indignity of his mother's behavior.

"I didn't because it was your mother that sent the invite to your grand opening that brought us back together," she said, pressing a hand to his chest.

"Doesn't change the fact that to interfere in the lives of her sons like that is nothing but hubris and ego." Cole's voice chilled as his anger resurfaced.

Forgiving was far easier than forgetting.

"I agree," Gabe said, tossing the rest of his skewer onto his plate as if his appetite had vanished.

Or been taken from him by his annoyance.

"I wonder what other secrets we're clueless to," Gabe muttered.

Cole thought of the huge one he carried about his father. He felt guilt at his complicity.

"Monica…" Gabe said.

Cole looked over at her face. She shifted nervously, and was avoiding his brother's eyes. It was odd and telling.

Uh-oh.

"At this point, anything you are keeping from me is a betrayal," Gabe said, his voice hard.

She closed her eyes and released a heavy breath. "But I signed a nondisclosure agreement when I was hired," she said.

Uh-oh.

Cole could only imagine the things Monica knew about the family, having worked as their housekeeper for five years. The NDA had been necessary. Like it or love it, they were famous and the press—

the paparazzi—hungered for a break in the armor that shielded the family's privacy.

"Gabe…" he said, realizing she was in a terrible position.

"Monica," Gabe repeated sternly, ignoring his brother and keeping his laser focus on his bride-to-be.

"You can't say anything," she insisted, finally leveling her eyes with his.

Cole was curious.

"I once found a file in your parents' bedroom of all the brothers being under surveillance by a private investigator," she admitted, her words rushed and almost tumbling upon each other.

"What!" the men roared in unison.

If they had been in a cartoon, the walls and floors would have shaken.

Monica squeezed her eyes shut then opened one to look back and forth between them.

Gabe angrily paced.

Cole's grip on his wineglass threatened the fragile stem.

"Maybe it's time to flush out their secrets and give them as good as they give," Cole said, curious if his father's dalliances had continued over the years.

Gabe paused and looked over at his brother. "I wonder how much they would like a PI digging into their lives," he said. "I can't even believe the nerve of them. Our parents. Are we that big of a sheep to them that *we* deserve no privacy?"

Cole felt insulted. Indignant. Betrayed.

Again.

That stung.

And he was sick of it.

"Well, an investigator helped me with locating my mother," Monica said, referring to her trials to reconnect with parents who had given her up into the foster care system.

"What was her name again?" Gabe asked. "Bobbie…?"

"Barnett," she supplied.

"Are we doing this?" Gabe asked.

Cole firmly nodded. "Hell yeah."

One week later

Jillian was relieved to enter her apartment. It was nearly midnight. She was bushed and thankful to have the next day off. The restaurant's renovation and more updated look had increased bookings and the entire night she and her team had been swamped with orders. During the work, the fatigue had been beaten off with energy, a desire to perfect and a need to please each patron. Afterward, without work to fuel her, exhaustion was queen.

She eased everything to the floor by the closed front door, including the clothes she wore. Naked, she freed her topknot and shook her curls out as she made her way down the hall to her bedroom. Not even the pastel colors against a white backdrop gave her their usual boost as she entered the en suite bathroom and treated herself to a quick shower and washed her hair to free it of the smell of food clinging to her.

Once done, she stood in the shower and inhaled deeply of the steam now scented with her favorite soap and shampoo. The only thing she had left to do for the night was to call Cole. Looking forward to seeing his face and hearing his deep voice spurned her to open the fogged door to step out and wrap a plush white towel around her damp hair and then her body.

She retrieved her phone from her bag by the door. Quickly made her way back to the bedroom to sit cross-legged on the foot of the bed. She had missed calls and texts.

She chuckled at the funny meme her grandmother had sent of the sensual silver-haired man from the Dos Equis commercial—the most interesting man in the world. Ionie thought he was one of the sexiest men in the world and made no qualms about it.

Her father just wanted her to know he missed his daughter.

Her mother wanted a recipe for a meal to cook for her father for their upcoming anniversary.

Warren requested a call back when she had time.

With plans to call her family and friend the next day. Jillian returned Cole's missed call instead. She struck several cute poses as she waited for him to answer. She was disappointed when he never did.

Maybe he's asleep, she thought as she rose to plug the power cord into her phone before setting it on the turquoise-tinted glass bedside table.

Cole had always insisted she call to let him know she'd made it home safely. It would be the first night since her return from the east coast that he hadn't answered. She turned off the clear globe lamp and dropped the towel around her body to the floor before climbing under the covers, enjoying he feel of the cool, crisp sheets against her skin as she looked out the window at the half moon. Snuggling one of her plump pillows to her side helped in how much she missed Cole's body beside her, but not by much.

Never had she expected to long for him in her life. Love had not been a part of her plan, but here she was. And she loved him.

His humor.

His smile.

His advice.

His loyalty.

His strong hugs.

His kisses.

His lovemaking.

She pressed her thighs and knees together as the bud nestled beneath the lips of her intimacy swelled with life. Some attention from his clever tongue was just what she needed to send her into a deep sleep. Cole's loving was the epitome of the Energizer bunny.

And of her fear of being hurt.

It lingered but was repeatedly defeated as her methods at wooing him seem to succeed. Cole seemed more like himself. Fun, charming, and with a ready smile.

The job at CRESS III was affording her choices— more than she'd had in a long time. She was steadily paying down her insufferable debt, helping her parents with her grandmother's in-home nursing care, and able to treat herself a little. The job didn't bring her the same freedom and joy of working for herself, but the stability it offered was clear.

And after financial ruin, that was important.

Bzzzzzz. Bzzzzzz. Bzzzzzz.

Her heart jolted at the sudden loud vibrations of her phone against the glass. She flopped over to snatch it up and smiled at *his* contact picture on the screen. She answered. "Hey, Cole," she said, touching the globe to illuminate the bedroom some.

He gave her the grin that made all her pulses race. "You in bed already?" he asked.

"Not sleeping," she assured him, feeling a tiny niggle of shock at how accommodating she was willing to be for him.

The Jillian of old had only cared about having her sexual appetited sated.

The new territory in which they'd ventured was still a little frightful because she was phobic of love.

But the feeling of being in love was beautiful. Nicer than she had ever thought or imagined it to be.

Will he ever admit to loving me back? Does he?

"Wait? Where are you headed?" she said, noticing when the phone dipped that he was fully dressed— leather jacket and all.

"Open the door."

She sat upright as her heart hammered and her stomach tightened. "Huh?" she said softly, tentatively tossing the covers back from her body. "Don't joke. It's not funny."

Cole chuckled and the twinkle in his gray-blue eyes

against his shortbread-brown complexion was magnetic. "My bad. Sorry," he said.

She made a face and flopped back onto her pillows. "Got my hopes up, Cole Cress," she chastised him.

He just shrugged one broad shoulder.

Jillian arched a brow. "Wait. Huh?" she said as she straightened. "Are you here or not?"

"Am I?"

Jillian ended the call and rushed from her bed. Her bare feet lightly beat against the hardwood flooring as she rounded the corner, jetted down the hall, and snatched the front door open just as naked as the day her mother had pushed her into the world. But the hall was empty, and her disappointment stung.

Shoving the door to swing it closed, she turned. "I am going to tell Cole Cress something about tricking me!" she muttered, now in an intolerable lousy mood.

"Tell me to my face."

She spun.

Cole leaned in the doorway, his arm keeping the door from actually closing.

She covered her shock well and leaned against the wall to eye him. "You came this far, come a little bit more," she said in a sultry voice as she beckoned him with a wiggle of her index finger.

He nodded and hung his head for a moment before looking up to take in her nudity. His eyes smoldered and seemed to darken in color. "I flew across the country just to spend your day off with you," he countered.

A playful battle of wills.

"I can't believe you're here," she said, looking down

the length of the hall at him as she fought like hell not to run and collide into him.

"Meet me halfway," he offered.

Jillian pushed off the wall and slowly walked to the midway point between them. She loved how his eyes did not miss the sway of her hips or her breasts. She was already bold and confident, but his attention made her feel simply divine. And when he stepped inside to close the door, dropped his leather duffel bag and then all of his clothing to join her mess on the floor, she gave him the same ogling—enjoying every moment and movement of his strong muscled frame.

It was the sway of his member back and forth across his thighs that was her undoing, and she moved to him, taking the inches into her hand as he encased her in his embrace and tasted her lips with hunger as she stroked him to hardness.

Cole picked her up, and she clung to his neck, pressing kisses to his shoulder as she guided him to her bedroom.

Atop her on the middle of the bed, and in her deeply, he made fierce love to her. Her fears were quieted and she felt hopeful this man—this beautiful, loyal and charming man—would be hers.

Long after explosive climaxes that had evoked cries from them both, she lay against his chest with her bent legs atop his and enjoyed the up and down movement of his chest as he took deep breaths meant to sustain him after such an exhaustive workout.

"What will we do tomorrow?" Jillian asked as she stroked her thumb across one of his flat brown nipples.

Cole lightly rested a hand on her buttocks and gave it a tap as he pressed a kiss to the top of her head. "Whatever you want. I just have a Zoom meeting with my team around nine, and then I'm yours for the rest of the day," he said, his deep voice seeming to rumble in his chest against her ear.

And hopefully for longer than that.

That thought caused her to stiffen in surprise. Love for Cole—she had accepted that fact. But more? Marriage? Forever? That was new. And startling.

"How's the revamp coming?" she asked, seeking a hiding place from her thoughts.

"Great, actually," Cole said. "When I took the position, it was more about family duty and obligation, but I have to admit my mother saw something in me that I am just discovering. I am enjoying the work and have a good eye for it. I want to succeed. Not to best my brothers for the CEO position my father will vacate, but to help make the best for whichever of my brothers succeeds him."

Cole. Ever loyal. And expecting nothing less. Even from her.

I will never let you down again, my love.

She rose slightly to look down at him and stroked the side of his face. "So, you've decided you don't want it?" she asked.

"I never did, but I'm ready now to officially step down from being in the race," he said before turning his head to press a warm kiss to her palm. "I'm learning that focusing on antagonizing my father is foolish.

Perhaps in my need to best him, I am worried I will become him."

She kissed the side of his mouth and fought the urge to declare her love for him even as it nearly burst her heart. She so badly wanted to ask for the impetus for his broken relationship with his father, but she refrained. Knowing how close she was to her parents, she couldn't imagine what had caused such a deep fracture between them.

"Whenever you want to talk about it, I am here for you," she whispered, needing him to know that she would always have his back.

Cole looked up and locked his eyes with her own. They searched hers for so long. So intensely. She could only hope that what he sought he found in her brown depths. "You are making this harder and harder for me," he admitted with the hint of a smile.

She tilted her head to the side, feeling hopeful. "Good," she whispered down to him.

One week later

The silence in Cole's now beautifully furnished living room was stunning as he, Gabriel and Monica sat on the low-slung, dark blue suede sofa and eyed the woman sitting across from them on the matching piece. Nothing echoed but the crackle of the modern slate fireplace to the side of them.

Bobbie Barnett, a medium-brown woman with long, wild, loose ebony curls that floated beyond her shoulders, long black lashes and pouty lips glossed with brown, was beautiful. Still, it wasn't the private investigator's looks that held everyone captive.

It was the truth she'd just revealed to them.

"Well, damn," Gabe finally said, reaching for Monica's hand and holding it tightly.

Cole rose and walked over to the dining room, needing space and clarity. He hadn't known what secrets, if any, would be uncovered, but never had he expected to be told his father had an illegitimate son in England from when he was just eighteen. Before he'd even met their mother.

Another Cress son.

A brother.

What do we do with this information?

"What's his name?" Gabe asked.

Cole turned and crossed his arms over his chest as he awaited the response.

"Lincoln Cress," Bobbie offered, her voice soft and raspy.

Cole frowned. "Did he know? Our father. Did he know?" he asked, striding across the room to rejoin them.

Bobbie sat back and crossed her legs. "At this point, I doubt it. His name is on the birth certificate, but it's not signed," she said, opening the file she held in her lap. "I have a little info on your brother. On Lincoln. Do you want it?" She eyed them all.

Gabe and Monica shared a brief look.

Cole released a deep breath as he glanced at his booted feet and then back over to her. "I do," he admitted.

"Me, too," Gabe agreed.

Bobbie nodded and tossed her wild mane behind her shoulder as she cleared her throat. She removed a photo and set it on Cole's wide metal-trimmed stone coffee table. "He lives in England where he is a chef at his own Michelin-star restaurant," she said, pausing to look up at them at the similarity. "Single. No children. Well off. Well educated. And upon meeting him, without revealing to my true intent in being there, he is... uh...quite a character."

Cole reclaimed his seat and took the photo Gabe had studied and then handed to him. "Meaning?" he asked before looking down.

Their eldest brother resembled Lenny Kravitz. In good shape. Strong features. Handsome.

He could see similarities in this stranger and their father.

"A little moody," she said with an expression that made it clear their encounter had not been fun for her. "*Rude* comes to mind, but perhaps I caught him at the wrong time. Who knows?"

"I think we need to know more about him before we even decide what to do next," Cole suggested.

"I would recommend a blood test at some point," Monica offered.

The brothers nodded in agreement.

Bobbie set the folder on the table. On top was her bill, including fees for her trip to England. "I think it entails a trip back to London to really get at it," she said.

Neither man flinched at the hefty price or the next bill to come.

"Fine," they said in unison.

She rose and offered her hand to all three. "Good. We can do it week to week and, whenever you tell me it's enough, I'm headed home," she promised. "Don't worry, I won't charge extra for his bad mood."

Monica walked the other woman to the door while Cole and Gabe shared a long look as neither could do anything more than release heavy breaths.

Eight

One month later

"Six months," Jillian said, standing in front of the mirror and eyeing her reflection in her black T-shirt and matching uniform pants.

She'd given the position half a year and she still hated it. Not the ability and desire to cook delectable meals—that was an inherent part of who she was and had always longed to be. The rules of the corporate structure left her feeling restricted and her culinary gift now felt a burden.

For Cress, INC. to be started by two world-renowned chefs who had a bevy of sons, also just as skilled and well known in their field, was particularly irksome for her. Phillip Senior and Nicolette should understand more than anyone with just a business background that chefs needed the freedom to create, to evolve.

The decision to add a varying seasoning was watched over by the manager with the eye of an eagle—or more like a buzzard awaiting its next prey to fail and fall to its death.

Jillian made a playful face before turning from her reflection. Quickly she grabbed her phone and her satchel, being sure her beloved engraved knife set was snuggled inside it. At the door, she retrieved her short, lightweight, black trench from the closet and then walked out the door. She considered driving the short distance to the restaurant but walked instead, enjoying the smell of the harbor. She released a breath and eased her hands into the deep pockets of her trench coat. Inside one was an envelope. She stroked it with her fingers. She'd debated what to do with the letter ever since she'd written it, carefully folded it and sealed it inside. That had been a week ago.

It was her resignation.

Never had she felt such ill at ease about going to work. She knew the feeling to be dread. Creativity could not thrive in such an environment. Not even when her restaurant had begun to fail had she lost determination to get in and fight for her dream. Never had she thought of giving up.

Never.

But failure had taught her well. Spending profits and not saving them for possible bad times ahead had been so very foolish. *Never again*, she promised herself.

And, if she were honest, even the strict nature of

Cress, INC. had taught her something. About efficiency, marketing, low turnover, and the need for a team outside of making great meals, for a restaurant to thrive.

Her dread resurfaced as she eyed the towering restaurant at the end of the pier. The spacious parking lot was empty, save the section set aside in the rear for employees. She rolled her eyes at the sight of Clark's yellow vintage Mercedes-Benz parked in his spot next to her empty one.

Her hand stroked the envelope again.

She had been diligent in paying down her debt and even had some money saved. All would not be lost if she used the six months of experience and took it to another restaurant or tried again at opening her own.

The last thought slowed her steps just as she reached the rear door leading directly into the kitchen.

Am I better prepared this time?

She sighed.

That, she didn't know. But what she was sure of was the feeling that she was missing out on so much by sticking it out in San Francisco. Her man. Her family. Her creative freedom.

It was not just the structure and conformity she disdained. Not being in New York with Cole and her family felt like a waste when she was so unhappy without them.

But what about my dreams?

Her grandmother had longed to teach. She had done so until she'd reached retirement age.

Her mother had yearned to marry her "Bear" and have a child. She had. Devoted herself to it. She hadn't gone to work until Jillian had graduated high school.

Now she worked as a clerk at the county courthouse, but marriage and motherhood had been her everything.

Her father's love of cars was bred from childhood and now he was an auto mechanic for a dealership. Another dream realized.

Cole threw his all into everything. Be it his love of motorcycles, his food truck, or now a desire to succeed at his position at Cress, INC.

If I run home to them while they have lived their dreams, am I giving up too easily on my own?

Jillian turned and leaned against the rear of the building, looking up at the afternoon sun.

Maybe it is time for a new dream...

"Good afternoon, Chef."

She looked over and smiled at one of the waiters walking up to the restaurant to begin his shift.

"Afternoon," she said just as her phone vibrated inside her pocket. She removed it and looked at the screen.

Cole.

She swiped to answer his call. *"Bonjour Monsieur Cress. Ça fait plaisir d'avoir de tes nouvelles?"* she said, trying to use the French he was teaching her to let him know it was good to hear from him.

He chuckled. "Not bad."

"Considering you only taught me that and how to demand you get naked for me," she added.

"Say it."

"Rends-toi nu pour moi," she said, enjoying seeing his handsome face smile with pride.

"I wish I was somewhere private and then I would," he assured her, his voice deep and delicious to her ears.

Jillian paused in making a naughty comment at all of the bustling activity behind him. "Where *are* you?" she asked.

"Checking in on the preparation for the launch party tomorrow night." He looked back over his shoulder.

"Oh," she said.

He faced his phone again. "What's wrong?" he asked, knowing her so well.

"Nothing," she said.

Not getting an invite to the event was the side effect of their secret affair. She wanted nothing more than to buy a beautifully sexy gown and attend.

"You're more than welcome, Jillian," he said, as if reading her thoughts. "I didn't want to put you in a position to have to choose between having me or having your job…again."

She forced a smile and nodded. "But what if I chose you?" she asked.

He looked surprised.

"Would you have me at your side as your guest? Your date?" she asked, hating that she wasn't sure he would.

His face became serious. "Without question."

Warmth spread over her chest.

"Then I do have a choice to make," she said, refraining from sharing with him another sentence she was teaching herself via her phone's translator.

Je t'aime de tout mon cœur.
I love you with all my heart.

Cole rubbed his hands together before checking his watch as he stood near the grand ballroom entrance of

the luxury Manhattan hotel. He felt pride as he sur-
veyed the crowd enjoying the lush party décor, open bar,
and abundance of heavy appetizers as they listened to
upbeat music and conversated. Tuxedos and sparkling
gowns were in abundance. Press and peers were awaiting the new interactive website's relaunch at midnight—
a costly feat he was confident was worth every cent.

He wiped his hand over his shadow of a beard and
then smoothed his hands down the front of his dark
navy tuxedo and matching shirt. He was surprised by
his nervousness. Although they practiced the count-
down to the launch numerous times, a flop at this point
would be disappointing and embarrassing,

"Don't worry, you look amazing, and you know it."

He turned to find Barbara, a member of the Cress,
INC. office staff, walking up to him with two glasses
of champagne in her hands. She used to make sublimi-
nal advances to his brother Gabe before his relationship
with Monica had ruled the papers once the former maid
had inherited millions after the death of the famous father she had never known.

Barbara now gave Cole the extra touch and long
looks.

In the past, he would have taken the invite and found
a private space to give her the release she sought. Things
were different. He was different.

Because of Jillian.

"No, thank you, Barbara," he said with emphasis as
he eyed the glass—and whatever else—she offered him.

She arched a brow and shrugged a bare shoulder in her

strapless dress before drinking one flute of champagne and then the other before turning and walking away.

He was glad to see her leave him be.

"Mr. Cress."

He turned to find a waiter holding a tray. A small envelope sat upon it. He knew as he reached for it that it was from Jillian.

She's not coming.

"Thank you," he said to the young server.

He held the envelope, letting his disappointment set with him. He had wanted her there but hadn't wanted to pressure her. His position at the door was not just to greet his guests but to ensure he saw her as soon as she stepped into the party.

Cole recognized her handwriting on the envelope and stroked his name as he strolled away from the door. He had taken a few steps and paused. "Wait," he said.

How would a handwritten note from Jillian even get there if she was thousands of miles away?

He opened the envelope and removed the note. "'You are the sexiest man in the room. No question,'" he read aloud.

He turned. Then he smiled.

Jillian stood in the hall outside the ballroom, looking stunning in a chocolate cami maxi dress cut on the bias with a deep vee and thin straps. A delicate brown lace jacket, worn open, trailed behind her, perfecting framing her sultry body in the clinging silk. Her normally curly hair was pulled back into a sleek ponytail; her eye makeup was dramatic and her lips were covered in a nude gloss.

Beautiful, he mouthed, clutching her note as he walked over to her.

As he stood before her with his heart thundering at a frenzied pace and his entire body electrified by her very presence, he would be even more a fool to deny his feelings for her. They consumed him. They pushed him to reach for her and pull her body to his kiss as he lowered his head and feasted of her lips. The moan he released was pure hunger.

He broke their kiss with reluctance and looked down at her. "All your gloss is gone," he said.

She shrugged as she reached up to wipe the remnants of it from his mouth. "To *hell* with that gloss," she said.

"I'm feeling like to hell with this party," he said, his inches swelling to life.

"And miss your big moment? Never." Jillian lifted on her heels to taste his mouth.

"I'm having another big moment right now." Cole looked down at his rising erection.

"Oh, big indeed," she said with a sassy wink.

They laughed.

"So, I made my choice, Cole. I chose you," she said, pressing her hand to the side of his face.

"Me wanting you here was never about proving anything. I just wanted you by my side. Enjoying your company. Feeling your support. Dancing with you in my arms as I celebrate. Seeing you cheer me on," he admitted with total honesty.

Her eyes softened.

It struck a chord in Cole that rang loudly.

"But my mother will not be pleased," he said.

"The choice is hers," Jillian said, stepping back to open the small gold clutch hanging from her wrist.

He looked on as she replaced her lip gloss and checked her hair in the mirror of a compact. "Ready?" he asked when she snapped it closed and dropped it back in her purse.

She nodded.

He extended his hand and she slid hers into his. "Did you ever think we would be walking into a gala hand in hand together?" he asked as they entered the ballroom.

She chuckled. "Definitely not, *but* definitely happy to have been wrong," she assured him.

He raised the entwined hands and kissed the back of hers. He felt her shiver.

She closed her lace overlay to cover her breasts. "Hard nipples," she explained. "Don't want to poke anyone's eyes out."

He laughed.

Her humor was entertaining.

As he saw his parents moving toward them, he knew they would need it. "Here we go," he warned, bending to press a kiss to her temple.

Jillian's height seemed to rise a bit beside him and he knew she had straightened her back. He hated someone feeling a need to prepare themselves to match his mother, but he also knew the two women in his life were about to bump heads because of the deal they'd brokered about him.

Nicolette patted her gray-streaked blond updo as she gave them a perfect smile that was as fake as a fifty-dollar Hermès Birkin bag. "Hello, Cole. Your father and I weren't aware you were bringing a guest," she said.

"I wasn't aware that I needed to have a guest approved," he countered in a pleasant tone.

"Cole," Phillip Senior warned in a gruffly stern voice.

He eyed his father coolly. The desire to reveal his long-lost son to him dripped from his tongue. However, he refrained from the move for the love of his entire family and wanting to shield his mother still—as they awaited a new report from the private investigator.

When Phillip returned his look with a glare, Cole stepped into the familiarity of his anger and disappointment at his father, failing at growing beyond it.

"Needless to say. You're fired," Nicolette said to Jillian, her smile still in place as she looked around and waved at those whose eyes she found on them.

Jillian stopped a waiter, picked up two glasses of champagne and handed one to his mother. She reached into her clutch and removed her cell phone.

Cole looked on in curiosity as she dialed a number.

"Hello, Clark? Yes, this is Jillian. I'm here with Mrs. Cress—"

Clark? The manager of Cress III?

"Yes, *that* Mrs. Cress," Jillian said with a nod and lick of her lips. "Please confirm for her that I handed in my resignation, giving two weeks' notice, before I left last night."

Cole bit back a smile, loving her even more.

She put the phone on speaker. "Go ahead, Clark."

"I don't have time for your jokes, Jillian," he said, not believing her. "Some of us have to work."

"Cool. I no longer have time for you, Clark. You insufferable a-hole," she said. "Mrs. Cress just fired me, so you need to find a replacement ASAP. That two-week window just closed."

She ended the call and touched her champagne glass to Nicolette's.

Ding.

"Thanks so much for ending that even sooner than I thought," Jillian said with a bright smile.

Cole eyed his mother's face and was afraid she was going to have a stroke as her left eye seemed to blink uncontrollably.

"First Gabe and now you with this crap," Phillip Senior snapped.

"Exactly," Nicolette agreed with coldness.

And that pushed him to the limit. Seeing his parents judge and find Jillian unsuitable with such callousness was disturbing. So swiftly, he was reminded of the same disdain his father had expressed to Gabe when he'd first revealed that he was dating Monica.

There are women you wed and those you bed. Know the difference. And that goes for all of you. The anger Cole had felt back then was twofold now because it was Jillian his father was insulting.

"Jillian is the type of woman I can cherish and respect and be loyal to," he said, his eyes daring his father to say more. "A woman worthy of nothing but good, just like any other woman…including my mother."

His father's lips thinned to a line.

Cole was thankful for Jillian's tight grip on his hand as he was taken back to that moment the light he'd felt for his father dimmed all those years ago...

Cole hitched his book bag up higher on his thin shoulders as he climbed from the back of the family's limousine in the uniform of his private school. "Thanks, Franco," he said to their driver, who gave him a two-finger salute as he was surrounded by the loud and echoing sounds of Midtown Manhattan. Cole had boldly sneaked from home and left his brothers behind to finish their afterschool studies while he hoped to help out in the kitchen in any way during busy dinner service.

His older brother, Phillip, was the sous chef. Sean had just finished his studies in culinary arts at Le Cordon Bleu that summer in Paris and worked there, as well. Gabe, at seventeen, had just begun culinary school and assisted in the bustling kitchen whenever he was home. Cole, at fifteen, wanted in on the action. Since they were young, their famous parents had taught them how to cook and praised them often for their skills.

This was a bold move but anything worth savoring was worth the risk.

Cole jogged up the concrete steps to the wide double-glass doors. He entered, barely paying attention to the towering adorned ceilings and elaborate Art Deco décor as he made his way to the kitchen.

"Hey, Chef, it's one of your boys," the burly pastry chef, Victor, yelled out. "Which one are you?"

"Coleman," he offered as his mother walked out of her office to give him a curious blue-eyed stare.

"I completed my homework during school so that I could help out today," he offered, his words rushed as he walked over to her, already towering over her by a couple of inches.

Nicolette gave him a chastising look even as she pressed a kiss to his already chiseled cheek. "Mon beau fils rebelle," she said. My handsome and rebellious son.

He gave her a smile that already had girls sending him longing looks.

"Ask your father," she said with one last soft pat to his cheek before using the back of her hand to brush her blond bangs from her face.

He knew his mother would be easy. Up until she'd had Lucas, his little brother, he had been her undoubted favorite.

Cole moved to the sink to wash his hands, knowing his father would check because his rule was to wash hands as soon as any kitchen was entered. He felt nervous as he made his way through the large, bustling kitchen to the rear hall leading upstairs to a small apartment above the restaurant that his parents used as their joint office and storage.

He had already practiced his speech. "Dad, I finished my homework. Can I help out in the kitchen? Mom said it was up to you," he said, coming to a stop before the closed door.

Taking a breath and feeling confident, he reached for the knob and turned it before pushing the door open. His grip on the knob tightened as he eyed his father with his pants down around his ankles, rutting away between the open legs of some woman atop the desk.

It was more of his father than he needed or wanted to see.

Fueled by anger and bitter disappointment in a man who could do no wrong in his eyes, Cole rushed across the room and used both his hands to shove against his father's side with a savage grunt that only hinted at his hurt. He backed away as they cried out and rushed apart. The expressions on the faces of his father and on whom he now saw to be one of the restaurant's long-time waitresses were of shock.

As they struggled to correct their clothing, Cole turned and raced down the hall, then the steps, wishing he had never dared to come to work. Or gone up the stairs. Or opened the door.

Or had seen what he'd seen...

Things between them had changed at that moment.

Cole knew a huge part of his childhood had been lost by his discovery...and in keeping his father's betrayal a secret. "Judge not," he warned Phillip Senior before walking away with Jillian close at his side.

Hours later, Jillian rolled over in Cole's bed and found it empty. She raised her head from the pillow and looked around once her eyes adjusted to the darkness. He stood by the terrace doors, looking out at the cold, fall night, still naked. She allowed herself a lingering moment to enjoy the strong lines of his broad shoulders, defined back and buttocks before climbing from the bed. Sharing in his nudity, she crossed the room and wrapped her arms around him from behind as she pressed a kiss to his spine. He covered her arms with his own as if welcoming the comfort she gave him.

The launch and the party had been a glorious success, but she knew their heated interaction with his parents lingered, taking some of the shine from his event for him. Long after they'd returned to his condo and showered, he'd lain in silence in their bed. Not even seeking the explosive sex he usually craved.

"Why did you quit?" he asked, surprising her.

She frowned, now considering that her decision was a part of his worries, as well. "I didn't care for the structured format, and it was so hard to not be here in New York when I didn't even like it," she said, easing around his body to stand in front of him, pressing her back and buttocks to the cold glass. "Not that I couldn't use the money. It was the reason that I took the job in the first place."

"What?" Cole asked.

"I never told you, but I tried—and failed horribly—at opening my own restaurant," she said. "After my ego was blown up by social media and being a private chef to celebrities, I thought I was ready. I wasn't. And it ruined me financially. I was on a quest to rebuild and recover. And that job afforded me that, plus, I could help my parents with my grandmother's medical care."

He looked down at her and the light of the full moon highlighted his eyes. "You never told me that," he said.

She looked away. "It's embarrassing. Who wants to admit to crippling debt, a horrible credit score and starting over until I thought I had it all?"

Cole used a finger beneath her chin to tilt her face back to him. "So *why* did you quit?" he asked again.

To be here with you.

Fear kept her from speaking her truth. At that moment, her actions felt desperate, especially when she'd yet to succeed at getting him to proclaim loving her. But that was how she had truly felt. Lost without him. In a way she had never felt with any other man. Not even for her previous husbands.

Am I a fool? His fool?

"Jillian."

She avoided his electric gaze.

Cole lifted her body against the glass so that her eyes were level with his own. "Did you come back for me?" he asked, his voice so deep. So captivating. So stirring.

"Yes," she whispered, pressing her hand to the top of his strong shoulders.

The truth wouldn't be denied. Not any longer.

"You got me," he admitted, wrapping his arms around her naked frame and pulling her soft body against his formidable strength.

Her gasp was visceral. The first feel of his mouth on hers sent a thrill across her body as she wrapped her arms around his neck.

"You got me," he repeated against her lips as he carried them to the bed. "My Jillian. My beautiful Jillian. You got me, baby."

He pressed her body down onto the foot of the bed with his own. His hands cupped the sides of her face as he pushed her hair back and examined her as if cementing every detail to memory. His smile was slow and warmed his eyes as he continued to study her.

The look made her breathless. Anxious. Adored.

"My Jillian. You *got* me," he kept saying as he pressed light kisses to her forehead then her cheeks, her chin and, finally, her mouth. Slowly. As if to savor.

Never had she experienced anything more exquisite.

Cole deepened the kiss with their eyes locked as she released his sides from her gripping knees to spread her legs and gently thrust her hips upward. A tender urging. To enter her. Fill her. Please her.

He obliged with a slight shift of his hips to find her center with his tip.

"Cole!" she gasped just as he thrust inside her. Swift and deep. So deep.

The lips of her intimacy kissed his hardness and she clutched him with her walls.

His grunt of pleasure into her mouth was her reward.

There, on the foot of his bed, not sure they wouldn't tumble to the floor, they made love with aching slowness. Like a fine wine or a meal. Savored. Cherished. Needed.

Physically, it was familiar. Emotionally, it was all new. Different. Deeper. A fresh level of connection between them that shook her to her core. This was passion. Truly something she had never experienced before and could only hope to experience once again.

Cole placed his beautiful mouth near her ear. "Jillian," he whispered. "My Jillian."

Over and over again, captivating her.

She clung to him with her arms and legs, wanting him thrusting inside her forever. "Cole," she cried.

And when they trembled as they reached their climax together and their cries filled the air, Jillian knew that she was risking it all for her sexy rebel.

And he was worth it.

Nine

One month later

Cole's heart thundered as he quickly parked his motorcycle in the lot of the hospital. On the entire ride up on the elevator, he found it hard to stand still. He felt concerned and a need to be reassured that all was well. His stomach had been in knots since he'd gotten the call. As he received his visitor's pass and directions to the hospital room, he was ready for an update.

Another elevator ride took him to the third floor of the massive structure. As soon as the doors opened, he stepped off and moved to the nursing station. "Excuse me. Room 304, please," he said.

The nurse didn't look away from the computer as she held up her ink pen to cease further conversation.

"Girl, look up," someone said to the nurse whose name badge read "Olive."

And Olive did, leaning back a little in her seat as her emerald eyes took Cole in before she gave him a warm smile. "I'm sorry. What was your question?"

"Room 304, please," he repeated, his brows dipping slightly at how nearly all the eyes of the staff were on him.

Cole had no time to be eye candy.

"It's down the hall to the right," Olive said, pointing in that direction with her pen as she rose and leaned against the desk.

"Thanks," he said, turning to head off to where she'd pointed.

"No, thank *you*," Olive called behind him.

All thoughts of her and the giggling hospital staff were lost to him as he turned the corner. His steps faltered and then paused as he eyed Jillian and her ex-husband standing by the window. Warren was still in his scrubs and white coat.

Annoyance replaced Cole's worry. He wasn't surprised to see the man there at all. He worked in the hospital and, upon Jillian's return to New York, their friendship had continued. The cavemen DNA in him felt territorial and wanted to club the doctor. The evolved man who tried to respect his woman's relationships before him tried his best to keep the Neanderthal at bay.

But not successfully.

Cole grit his teeth, easing his hands into the pockets of the dark blue jeans he was wearing with a matching fisherman-knit sweater and brown leather boots. It's just that Warren's presence was becoming a norm. He seemed to always be in the mix. At her parents' house. On the phone. FaceTiming. Messaging funny memes.

He tried to reason that, before their marriage, they had been childhood friends.

Again, not successfully.

Jillian crossed her arms over her chest and leaned her head against the window as she looked out. His eyes shifted to Warren's tall figure. He frowned as the man looked at her profile with what appeared to Cole to be love and longing. Jillian chuckled and looked back up at him. Warren's expression instantly changed, keeping his feelings for her cloaked.

For him, his suspicions that Warren wanted to be her next and not just her ex were confirmed.

Jillian glanced down the hall and saw Cole. Her face filled with a light that warmed him as she came to him and seemed thankful for him to be there. He ate up the steps to reach her, wrapping her in his embrace and pressing a kiss to her forehead. "How's Ionie?" he asked.

"Stable," Jillian said, her arms wrapped securely around his waist as she looked up at him. "The doctor believes it was a stroke."

Tears filled her eyes and that wrenched his gut. "Hey, hey, hey," he said softly. "What I have learned about your grandmother is that she is a fighter. Right?"

Jillian smiled and bit her bottom lip. "I feel for the doctors when she's able to swing and wants to go home," she quipped.

They looked at each other and shared that kind of smile of intimacy and closeness.

He liked it a lot.

"I'm glad you're here. I need you with me," she admitted, pressing her hands to his back atop the sweater.

He raised her body up to lightly kiss her lips before setting her back down on her feet.

"Hello, Cole."

He stiffened and looked over Jillian's head at the other man. "Warren," he said, offering no warmth even as he gave him a forced smile.

Warren pushed his spectacles up on his nose and gave Cole a stiff smile, as well.

"Thanks for coming to check on my grandmother, Warren. You'd better get back to your rounds before you're missed," Jillian said as she released Cole and turned to her friend.

"Yeah, I gotta go. I have surgery in a little bit," he said, checking the time on his pager.

"She's in good hands," Cole reassured him as he placed his arm around Jillian's shoulders.

Warren nodded. "I'll check on you later," he said to her before walking away.

Keeping her grandmother's well-being paramount, Cole set aside his concerns about Warren's feelings for Jillian as they walked together to enter Ionie's hospital room.

"Good evening, everyone," he said, giving Jillian's parents a nod of greeting before moving to the side of the bed where Ionie looked less energetic.

She opened her eyes at the sound of his voice and then squeezed them shut. "Cole, you turn around until Jillie puts my lipstick on me," she said, sounding tired and talking slowly.

He chuckled and bent to press a kiss to her soft cheek. "Beautiful as ever," he said to her.

That made Ionie smile.

Jillian sat beside her grandmother on the bed. As Ionie kept them entertained with her quick wit, which wasn't harmed by her slow words, Cole eyed Jillian. Things between them were so serious. So intense.

So needing of ultimate trust and understanding.

But that wasn't easy for him, especially knowing her ever-present ex harbored love for her.

Over the years, he'd seen many relationships shatter because of infidelity—emotional and physical.

For so long, he had fought hard not to give in to the weakness that love could be. The vulnerability. The risk. The danger.

Does Jillian love Warren, as well? Is there more there that I'm missing?

His eyes shifted to Jillian's profile and his doubts gripped him.

He wanted it to work. He truly wanted them to be one of the few to make it.

His fear of betrayal just wouldn't allow him to believe it could be.

Jillian gently gnawed at her thumb as she swiped through online listings for chef positions, sitting at the kitchen table at her parents' house. Cole had taken them all to dinner after they'd left her grandmother to get some rest. Although she knew he wanted her to go to his condo, she had begged off to be with her parents instead.

When she was with Cole, she got too lost in him and would forget her anxiousness over being unemployed. Still. The last thing she wanted was to reveal to him that she had moments when she regretted leaving her well-paying job—mainly anytime she paid a bill and had to dip into her savings.

And now her grandmother's medical bills would increase; she would need physical therapy to fully regain her walking stature.

"Damn," Jillian swore, covering her face with her hands as she fought not to feel so overwhelmed by it all.

She'd chosen love, but love didn't pay the bills.

She picked up her phone and opened the text she'd received from Gunther Red, the award-winning musician, asking if she was available to chef for a two-week cruise around the Greek Isles. The money was great, the locale and freedom ideal, but his love of cocaine and pleading to see if she tasted as good as she looked had kept her from accepting.

Her thumb floated above the phone as she eyed the text and seriously considered dancing with—or rather avoiding—the devil for two weeks. Any hope his wife would help keep him from being handsy went out the window when the woman had made her advances for a threesome.

Jillian dropped the phone and ran both hands through her curls before gripping the soft hair in her fists.

Bzzzzzz. Bzzzzzz. Bzzzzzz.

She looked at her phone at the incoming text. Cole. She swiped to open it.

My Heart: I have a headache.

"Awww," she said as she picked up her phone to text him back.

Do you have a pain pill?

Bzzzzzz. Bzzzzzz. Bzzzzzz.

My Heart: Wrong head...

She laughed. The exchange reminded her of their no-strings sexual adventures when they would've been tearing each other's clothes off within an hour.

"What's so funny?"

Jillian set her phone down and looked up at her mother passing by her to wash her hands at the sink. "Nothing," she said. "Why are you up?"

Nora opened the fridge. "Your daddy got thirsty," she said, reaching in to pull out a bottle of water. "And why are you up? It's after one."

"Looking for a job," she admitted.

Nora looked at her as she eased the water bottle into the pocket of her fluffy, bright yellow robe. "You'll find something," she assured her. "You want me to take a look at your résumé?"

Jillian nodded. "Yeah, maybe so, Mom. Thank you. I'll email it to you."

"Good," Nora said, wrinkling her nose at her daughter affectionately before walking away.

Jillian picked up her phone, looking at both invites on her phone. One from the man she loved. The other from a man who seriously needed therapy and or drug rehab.

"Jillian."

She looked over her shoulder, surprised to find her mother standing in the archway. "Yeah?"

"What's going on with you and Warren?" Nora asked, coming back to take a seat at the table.

"Me and Warren?" Jillian balked, a frown on her face.

"Yes."

The women eyed each other.

"Nothing. Just friendship. I'm with Cole, remember?" she said, reaching over to playfully tug her mother's thumb.

Nora eyed her. Studied her.

Jillian's frown deepened.

"Just make sure *you* remember, dear," Nora finally said. "And if you want something else, that's okay, but always be clear with your intentions. It's less messy."

Jillian waved away her mother's concerns as she rose to retrieve her own bottle of water from the fridge. "Warren and I are just friends. Plus, Cole is a grown man who understands that. Trust me. I got this."

Nora grunted. It revealed her disbelief in just how much her daughter "had it."

"Night, Ma," she said, reclaiming her seat and picking up her tablet as her mother took her leave. She searched the internet for Gunther Red and within moments her decision was made. The most recent articles were about a woman claiming he'd held her captive during a drug binge.

"Oh *helllll* to the no." Jillian picked up her phone to politely decline the private chef gig.

Dropping her phone back to the table, Jillian rubbed her bottom lip with her thumb.

Bzzzzz. Bzzzzzz. Bzzzzzz.

She picked it back up and opened the text from Cole. It was a picture of him in bed. Ready and waiting, if she was willing. She eyed him in all his rugged glory. It was quite a temptation.

Jillian grabbed her devices and turned the lights off in the kitchen before making her way up the stairs to the guest bedroom. It had been hers until she'd gone to college. She removed her warm and toasty fleece pajamas and took a steamy shower. Once dried and then lathered in scented lotion, she eased her body into a slinky satin slip of bright emerald. It fell to her feet as she pulled on gold heels. She freed her curls from a messy topknot to arrange with nimble fingers before glossing her lips. Once she covered her sexy attire with a fluffy ostrich coat in the same green, she grabbed her phone and keys. As she prepared herself for yet another round of passion, the feel of the satin against her nudity was foreplay itself.

She felt sexy. Powerful. And she wanted him. Around her. On her. In her.

Jillian opened the front door and the late fall winds whipped around her, breezing her curls back from her face and tightening her nipples into buds that pressed through the thin material. She paused at the sight of a Mercedes-Benz Sprinter slowing in front of the house.

Cole.

In yet another of his vehicles he rarely drove.

He lowered the window just as surprised to see her leaving her parents' home as she was to see him pulling up in front of it. She came down the three levels of stairs, ignoring the cold, as she felt the heat of desire rise in her. She motioned with her head for him to park in the driveway.

He did.

When she neared the luxury van with its dark-tinted windows, the side door slid open. Cole was already sitting in the middle of the rear seat, in all black, his knees wide and his lap ready.

She stepped aboard and let her coat slide down her body to puddle at her feet as he closed the door and shuttered them from the frosty air.

He swore as he watched her with his beautiful eyes hooded as she came up the wide aisle to stand before him. His hands gripped her hips and then eased around to cup her soft buttocks. "I was just about to text you to come downstairs," he said, looking at her as she eased up the skirt of her slip to reveal she was bare beneath it before straddling his hips.

"And I was headed to bring it you," she whispered against his open mouth before lightly stroking her tongue against his bottom lip.

Cole trembled as he eased a hand over the curve of her bottom to slide his middle finger inside her core. He cried out at the wet feel of her.

Jillian tore at the button and zipper of his pants, glad when he raised his hips for her to jerk them down to his thighs. She freed his hardness. It was hot in her hands as she stroked him from the base to the smooth tip.

Cole sucked one of her nipples into his mouth through the material.

She arched and let her curls tickle her back and shoulders as he wrapped an arm around her waist. He lifted her with ease just to settle her back down on his lap, his hardness inside her.

With a wildness intensified by their desire and their locale, they got lost in their explosive heat and clung to one another as their bodies moved in sync for a fast and furious ride that just had to rock the luxury vehicle on its very wheels.

Cole sat back in his desk chair and crossed his legs as he eyed his brother reading the lengthy report Bobbie Barnett had sent them. He straightened the hem on his lined slacks as he waited for Gabe to finish the full story of their father meeting the mother of their half-brother Lincoln when Phillip was just eighteen and headed off to college. It included a background history on Lincoln and his mother. No stone had been left unturned.

"Bobbie's thorough," Gabe said, closing the file and looking up at his brother across his desk in his office at Cress, INC.

"Well worth the costly price," Cole agreed, shifting his watch on his wrist and arranging the sleeve of his tailored shirt to ensure it showed.

At Gabe's continued silence, Cole looked up to find his brother eyeing him oddly. "What?" he asked.

"Nice threads," Gabe said, failing at an attempt to keep from chuckling.

Cole stood and pulled the ebony tailored blazer over his matching shirt. He latched the lone button as he came from behind his desk to turn this way and that to show off his new suit. "Jillian suggested I look a little more professional coming to work," he said, raising his chin as he tightened the knot of his tie.

"Ah, the power of a pussycat," Gabe said, stroking his beard. "And stop primping. You're acting like Sean."

Now that made Cole howl with laughter. It was undeniable that their older brother, who favored the actor Daniel Sunjata, was the star of the family and knew it. In fact, he enjoyed starring in several of the culinary shows Cress, INC. produced, was friends with high-profile celebrities, and had been named one of *People*'s Top Ten Sexiest Chefs twice in a row. The charmer was as handsome and famous as he was a genius in the kitchen. And Sean knew it.

"Besides, I've seen you in a suit before, egomaniac," Gabe drawled, setting the file atop his brother's desk.

"Yes, but never in the office," Cole pointed out before removing the blazer and reclaiming his seat.

"Short of a DNA test to confirm things, it seems Lincoln Cress is indeed our brother," Gabe said.

"Our eldest brother," Cole corrected him.

Gabe shook his head and winced. "Phillip Junior won't like that."

Good.

Of all the Cress brothers, Phillip Junior was the most competitive and backbiting. He held an outdated belief that as the eldest son of the Cress family, he should be the undisputed heir to the company's throne. Learning that Phillip Senior had instead opened the opportunity up to all his sons had created a divisiveness among the brothers that was unsettling.

Cole removed his wallet and money clip from his pocket and counted off enough crisp hundred-dollar bills to cover his half of Bobbie's bill.

Gabe took the cash. "I'll cut her a check today," he said.

Cole nodded and rested his elbow against the arm of his chair before propping his chin in his hand. "Everyone needs to know about this," he began, thinking of the secret already weighing him down. "We have to call a family meeting."

"Do we speak to our parents alone or tell everyone at once?" Gabe asked. "You know, as hard as he has been on us, he was there every day—raising us, teaching us, reprimanding us. There are many things about our father that I doubt. But I know he loved being a father. Sometimes his sternness was this overreaching need to be for us what his father was not for him."

Cole shifted his gaze out the window as he fought with whether to share's his father's infidelity—a part of his father's life that was not in that file from Bobbie Barnett. And thus he took little comfort in her report of his current faithfulness. "Let's think about it and make a decision soon," he said, reaching for the file to carry it across his office to the safe inside his closet.

"Another Cress brother," Gabe mused, shaking his hand before releasing a light laugh.

"Maybe," Cole declared, locking the safe and returning to his seat.

They locked eyes.

Of all the brothers, Cole was closest to Gabe, who was older than him by just two years. And he knew they were thinking the same thing.

"A thousand," Cole offered, reaching in his wallet for another ten bills.

Gabe nodded and stood to remove his platinum money clip to do the same. "He looks just like us, Cole. He's our brother," he said. "Face it."

"I'm not against it. I'm just not as sure as you. That's all."

Betting was their thing since childhood. Be it a guess on what was for dinner or whether one would win the charm of one pretty girl over the other. The brothers had brought the act into adulthood.

Cole gathered the bills and slid them into a Cress-monogrammed envelope, removing the paper strip to reveal the adhesive as he sealed it.

"I should have bet you that you and Jillian would fall in love," Gabe said, remaining standing as he slid his hands into the pockets of his gray three-piece suit.

Cole put the envelope in the top drawer of his desk. There was another already sitting there. He opened it. There was five thousand dollars inside. "Who says I'm in love?" he asked as he tried to remember the reason for the cash.

"Are you not?" Gabe countered.

He showed his brother the envelope. "Did we bet on something and forget?" he asked.

Gabe chuckled as he strolled to the door. "I didn't forget. I lost. Your launch went off without a hitch," he reminded him over his shoulder.

Well damn.

Cole moved the money from the envelope into his money clip. "Gabe," he called before looking up.

His brother paused in the doorway.

"Would it bother you if Monica was still best friends with her ex-husband?" he asked, alluding to his doubts for the first time aloud.

"Ouch," Gabe said before wincing. "Um, I'm a good man, but I'm not a perfect man, so I don't know how I would feel, *but* I'm happy as hell that I don't have to worry about that. *Also,* I do believe that if it's bothering you, you might need to admit what you feel for Jillian."

Gabe locked eyes with his brother. "I care about her," he confessed.

"I know," Gabe said with a smile before tapping the door frame and walking away.

The sounds of Beyonce's "All Night Long" echoed against the walls of Cole's condo as Jillian paused to do body rolls before checking on the baked macaroni and cheese in the stylish navy-blue Viking oven. In a great mood, she wanted to reward herself and Cole with a down-home Southern meal. The kind her grandmother Ionie taught her to cook before her entry into culinary school to excel at French cuisine. Baked turkey wings smothered in brown gravy with onion and peppers, chicken pilau rice, cabbage cooked down with fried pork jowls, the mac and cheese with five kinds of cheese, candied yams, and cornbread.

A Southern feast.

She paused, wondering if Cole had ever had a traditional Southern meal. She certainly had never prepared any for the Cress family when she'd been their chef. And it was well known that all of the Cress chefs favored French cuisine.

"Well, he's getting fed some tonight," she said, using silicone mats to remove the glass dish from the oven to set on a large trivet on the counter.

"Some what?"

Jillian looked up in surprise to find Cole walking into the dining room from the hall leading from his in-unit parking space. He held his suit jacket and house keys in hand. "Soul food," she said. "That 'down below the Mason-Dixon line' comfort food."

He crossed the spacious kitchen to press a kiss to her temple as he looked at the bevy of serving dishes on the countertops. "Looks good," he said.

"You ever had a spread like this?" she asked, bumping her bottom back against him as she removed lids to show off her skills.

"No…and good thing because I would have looked more like Lucas growing up," he said before opening his mouth as she offered him a spoonful of her candied yams.

"Your brother Lucas was chubby?" she asked in surprise. "Sure doesn't look it now."

Cole playfully swatted her bottom. "How does he look now?" he asked.

Jillian cut her eyes up to him as she sucked the rest of the yams from the spoon, playfully wiggling her shaped brows at him.

He laughed and picked her up by the waist to sit her atop the island before standing between her open legs.

"Don't worry, I have the Cress brother I want," Jillian reassured him. "Lucas who?"

All of the Cress men—including their father—were good-looking, but it was only Cole who had drawn her appreciative eye. From the moment she'd looked past his mother during her interview for the chef position and seen him standing there watching her, she had been caught up in the man's web. Trapped by his looks. Enticed by his flirtation. And hooked by his sex.

Cole kissed her mouth and squeezed the top of her thighs. "Why the big meal?" he asked, still tasting the sweetness of the yam's brown sugar, cinnamon and butter glaze on her lips.

"Good news. My grandmother finally got into the rehab facility we wanted…" Jillian began as she undid his tie and loosened the top buttons of his shirt.

"Excellent," Cole said, truly looking pleased with the next step in her grandmother's recovery.

"And I got a new personal chef position," she said.

"Congratulations, beautiful," he said with enthusiasm.

"For Warren," she added, leaning toward him to press kisses to his neck.

Cole leaned back. A scowl lined his handsome face.

Jillian was shocked. "What's wrong?" she asked.

He turned and strode over to the Bose sound dock on the glass table behind the sofa. Soon the sound of Beyonce stopped mid-falsetto-note abruptly. He began to pace back and forth in front of the fireplace.

Jillian slid down from the island to join him in the living room. "Cole, what's going on? What's this about?" she asked.

He stopped his movement and eyed her. "Which is it, Jillian?" he asked. "Do you not see that Warren loves you? Do you not care that he loves you? Do you want him to love you still? What?"

"Warren does not love me, Cole," she said, waving her hand dismissively.

And instantly remembered giving her mother the same gesture.

What's going on with you and Warren?

She also remembered the grunt her mother had given her.

That grunt had said so much without saying a thing.

"He loves you. He wants you. Now, where are you with this?" Cole eyed her across the divide.

Jillian was confused by his anger. "Wait. What?" she asked. "You want me to turn the job down? Stay unemployed? Stay strangled by new debt? Not work? What?"

Cole wiped his hand over his mouth. "I would never try to control you like that, but I would like for you to be aware enough to understand when you are putting yourself in a compromising position," he said.

"A *compromising* position," she scoffed.

Cole jerked the hem of his shirt from inside his pants as if feeling restrained by it.

"Don't be blinded by jealousy, Cole," she said, shaking her head in disbelief. "I didn't even know you had a problem with Warren."

"Blinded by jealousy?" he snapped.

"Yes," she insisted, turning to walk back into the kitchen.

Cole followed.

She ignored him as she removed plates, linen napkins and cutlery from the cabinets and drawers to set the dining room table.

"Do you want a relationship with your ex?" he asked.

"Which one?" she asked sarcastically as she breezed past him.

"Jillian," Cole said calmly.

She set the dishes down on the corner of the table and looked to him.

"Do you want a relationship with Warren?" he asked.

"Definitely not," she insisted. "I see him as nothing but a friend. Damn near a brother, if we hadn't made the mistake of crossing the line from friends to more."

"He doesn't feel the same," Cole insisted.

"You're wrong. You don't know him. You're assuming," she said, now focusing on setting the table. "As a matter of fact, you're wrong about me. Why *assume* I would be inappropriate with an employer?"

"You were with me."

That felt like a blow.

She looked at him again, fighting an urge to toss something at him. "Really, Cole?" she asked, her tone accusing. "I guess I spread it out for everyone right along with the meals. Right?"

Cole released a heavy, harsh breath before pressing his fingers to his closed eyes. "I didn't say that."

"You said a lot," she charged.

Cole shoved his hands into the pockets of his slacks as he leaned his tall frame against the wall. "And what would you do if you found out I wasn't wrong and Warren loves you and wants you back?" he asked, his voice low and deep.

She frowned. "He doesn't. Damn!"

"What if he did?" he countered. "Would you still take the job?"

"Yes," she asserted.

He nodded in understanding. "At first, I hated the idea of you working for him because I was worried that something would happen. That you would betray me in a way I can swear I would never do to you..." he began. "But now, more than hating you being around him, I pity him because it's cruel, Jillian, to be blind to his feelings for you and to continue to hang around him while actively ignoring the heart he wears on his sleeve. Hoping for more than friendship."

"So now you're looking out for Warren?" she asked in sarcasm and disbelief.

He shook his head. "I remembered the offer my mother made and how you had no clue that I had any feelings outside of sex for you," he said, a chill entering his tone.

She swung between frustration with his assumptions and annoyance at him, clinging to the past. "I thought we were beyond that," she said.

"So did I. I was wrong."

Stunned.

That was the only word for how she felt at that moment.

They stared at one another. Cole looked away first.

That stung.

"Maybe I should give you some space," she said, even as she desperately yearned for him to implore her not to go.

"Maybe we should give each other some space," he countered.

That hurt.

It also spurred her to want to be away from him. Quickly.

She moved around the apartment, gathering her things and fighting not to let one single tear fall.

"What about the food?" he asked, still leaning against the wall from where he'd crushed her heart.

Jillian released a bitter laugh. "Please don't push me to tell you what you can do with that food," she snapped before snatching open the front door and leaving, wishing she could slam it closed.

She leaned against the door and hyperventilated, seeking control and not finding it.

The crash of dishes echoed through the solid wood and she froze at the shock. Turning, she pressed a hand to the door as she lowered her head.

What the hell just happened?

Ten

Two weeks later

"You ready, Cole?"

He looked up from the copies of Ionie's medical bills for her care at the rehab facility. Bobbie Barnett had been able to retrieve the paperwork for him, along with the accurate information on where to send payment. "One sec," he said as he opened his checkbook and paid in full the substantial bill that remained after the contribution by her medical insurance. He sealed the envelope and left it in his tray for outgoing mail that his assistant would ensure was handled.

In his and Jillian's brief time in a formal relationship, Cole had forged a cute relationship with her grandmother, Ionie, and he no longer wanted that financial burden on her or her family. A minimal loss to him could change the very fiscal outlook of their lives, and that didn't sit well with him.

And Jillian would be none the wiser. He had already included a request for anonymity.

They hadn't spoken since that day in his condo, and the last thing he wanted was for her to believe his gesture was a move to reconcile. He missed her, but his doubts about her relationship with Warren lingered. Be it she was complicit in the man's love for her or uncaring of it, neither was to his liking. Both hit too close to home with his own issues.

It was why he'd resisted serious relationships in the past.

"Ready," he said, grabbing his cognac leather bomber to pull over the navy dress shirt and denims he wore with polished brown boots. As the brothers walked together to the elevator, Cole removed a navy fitted sweater cap to cover his head and ears from the biting cold of winter outdoors.

"Welcome back." Gabe eyed Cole's return to more casual attire.

"Thank you," he said as they rode the elevator down to the lobby. "Now, if the weather will magically warm up so I can get some hours in on my food truck, I will be a very happy man."

"No, you won't," Gabe said as they strode across the massive, busy, sky-lighted lobby and through the automated glass doors of the Midtown Manhattan building.

Cole said nothing in response. There was nothing to

say. It was true. He was miserable without her. Again. And this time at his doing.

The brothers climbed into the rear of one of the company's vehicles as the driver held the door open for them. "Thank you," both said to Harvey.

They fell silent as Harvey reclaimed his seat and eventually pulled away from the parking spot in front of the building. The mood was tense. Neither was looking forward to this visit to the Cress family townhouse.

It was time for the truth to be revealed.

Cole looked out the tinted window at the city as they neared the prominent and historic Lenox Hill section of Manhattan's Upper East Side. His brother was silent as well, the investigative file resting on his lap. But Cole didn't bother to wager what occupied Gabe's thoughts. He was too focused on his own.

This will not go well.

The driver slowed the SUV to a stop in front of the five-story, ten-thousand-square-foot townhouse. Both men opened their rear doors and exited before Harvey could. "Give us an hour," Gabe said as Cole stood on the pristine sidewalk and looked up at the towering structure.

For such a huge part of his life, it had been home.

Now he was a visitor.

He opened the wrought-iron gate to jog up the steps, glancing back as his brother did the same. He rang the bell.

"Where's your key?" Gabe asked, reaching into the pocket of his camel wool coat.

"Respect is earned when respect is given," Cole explained. "Do you want our parents to feel they can just stroll into our home whenever they please?"

Gabe made a face. "You're right," he said, releasing the key back into his pocket.

"Ain't I always?" Cole asked.

Gabe volleyed back. "Not lately."

Another Jillian reference.

"I'm regretting talking to you about her," Cole said just as the elaborate front door opened.

Felice, the new housekeeper, smiled as she stepped back to pull the door wide for them to enter the marbled vestibule. "Hello, Mr. Cress and Mr. Cress," she said. "It's good to see you both."

They gave her warm smiles in greeting before walking the length of the entry hall to step into their parents' lavish, spacious living.room in its shades of light gray and steel-blue against the pale walls.

"Your coats?" she asked, already extending her arm.

Each removed his outer gear and turned it over to her.

"Mr. Cress is awaiting your arrival in the library," Felice said before turning to hang their coats in the closet. "Everyone is in their suite, preparing for dinner."

As the men made their way across the hardwood floor to the open kitchen and den area, Cole's steps slowed as he remembered the excitement he'd felt at knowing Jillian worked there. He had enjoyed teasing and flirting with her as much as when he'd finally bedded her. He smiled at the closed pantry door, pleased no one knew just how much fun he and Jillian had shared in there.

She was gone. A short and plump man in a red chef's coat was in her place.

The brothers rode the elevator upstairs to the second floor, where the movie theater and library were located. His parents occupied the entire third floor as their private suite, complete with a sitting room, massive walk-in closets, their joint home office, a pantry, and a spa bath. On each of the fourth and fifth floors, a huge den centered three-bedroom suites and another well-stocked pantry.

There was no denying the beauty of the home flushed with luxury and every creature comfort to be desired.

Cole and Gabe shared a last look before the elevator slowed to a stop.

Their father stood near the rear glass wall that ran the entire exterior of the home. He glanced over his broad shoulder to eye them before he turned. "Come in, boys," he said, his deep voice booming without even trying.

As they neared him, Cole saw his father's eyes dip to the file Gabe held. He didn't miss the way Phillip Senior rolled his shoulders back as if to steel himself.

"Are you staying for dinner?" Phillip Senior asked. "Chef is preparing Peking duck. I haven't had it in years."

"Listen, Dad, this is not an easy conversation to have, but it has to happen..." Gabe began, sitting in one of the leather armchairs and waving an invite to their father to take one of the seats across from him.

"Getting right to it?" Phillips Senior said with a

chuckle. "I assume the file is the reason the two of you requested this private meeting that we couldn't have at the offices."

Cole eyed him, searching for the love and respect he'd once held for him years ago. "Did you have people in the family followed by a damned private investigator?" he asked with a hard stare.

"Cole!" Gabe snapped.

He had just blown their carefully crafted plan out of the water.

Phillip Senior did take the seat before looking over at Cole, who was still standing. "I should have known with *your* involvement, niceties would be amiss," he said.

"The question still stands," Cole said, summoning the same strength he wished he'd had that day when he had just run from the restaurant and walked home.

"When will the hate fade, son?" Phillip Senior asked.

Cole's emotions tightened his throat. "I wish I hated you, then I wouldn't be so damn disappointed."

Gabe remained silent as if sensing a long-overdue moment between his brother and his father.

Some emotion he couldn't identify crossed Phillip Senior's broad face. He cleared his throat and shifted in his seat. "I never hired a private investigator in my life," he said.

Cole turned from him, trusting nothing he said to be the truth.

"Well, we did," Gabe said.

Cole glanced back just as his brother leaned forward

to sit the file on the table between them. "We felt you were deserving because you pried into our lives—"

"I did not!" Phillip Senior shouted.

"Regardless, we have discovered something that you need to know."

Cole turned to face them as Gabe removed his hand from the file and sat back.

"You have a son, Lincoln—"

"Lies!" Phillip Senior roared, jumping to his feet and swatting the file away with the back of his hand. "How dare you accuse me of such a lie! Is that what you think of me, Gabe? I know *he* hates the very air I breathe but do you believe that of *me*?"

Cole released a bitter chuckle. "Ask me, do I believe it after walking in on you screwing a waitress while our mother was downstairs in the restaurant," he said, his words dripping with contempt and his eyes stinging with the heat of his anger.

"What?" Gabe stormed in shock.

Phillip Senior pushed his chair onto its side before taking two large steps across the floor to lunge at Cole. He grabbed the front of his shirt in his fists. "You don't know what the hell you're talking about!" he yelled in his face, spittle flying.

Cole released another bitter laugh before his eyes went cold. "Liar," he said in a quiet voice that was damning.

Gabe squeezed between them and pushed to put distance between them. "Enough," he said.

"More than enough."

The three men swung their heads in the same direction to find Nicolette standing at the top of the stairs. Each man's chest heaved from emotion and exertion. They each turned and walked away from one another, seeking the control they had lost. Silence reigned, but the tension was omnipresent.

Cole moved to stand at the rear wall and look out at the snow beginning to fall and coat the backyard below. His eyes went to the garden Jillian had begun and how it had been taken over by weeds and overgrowth.

Neglect had a way of doing that.

He let his forehead rest on the cold glass. His heavy breaths fanned it. He had denied himself Jillian's attention and was beginning to feel and look as abandoned as the garden.

A flash of blue against the glass caught his eye and he watched in the reflection as his mother went to his father's side. "I knew about the affair," she admitted, pressing a hand to her husband's cheek to stroke it lovingly.

Cole's eyes widened. It was his turn to be stunned. He turned to eye them—united and in love. He had been a fool, thinking he'd sheltered and kept her free from hurt when all the while she had long since given her husband the forgiveness Cole would not. He didn't know how to feel, but pleased was nowhere on the list of possibilities.

Cole turned from them and fought the urge to valiantly punch his fist through the glass until the entire rear wall shattered. Instead, he lightly tapped it against his leg.

"What affair? When?" Gabe asked.

"Fifteen years ago," Nicolette supplied as she guided Phillip Senior to another chair to sit.

"And did you know Cole knew about it?" Gabe asked. "Just how many secrets does this damn family have?"

"No, I didn't know Cole knew," Nicolette insisted.

That was of little reprieve.

"I've got to get out of here," he said.

Gabe blocked his path. "No! Don't run from it. Make them stand in their mess and realize it created more mess," he said before stepping past his brother to eye their parents. "You two have this weird bubble where first and foremost there's only the two of you. Even now, you comfort a man who betrayed you and ignore a son who protected you."

Nicolette look confused at first and then her expression changed as if Gabe's point of view was now her own. "My Cole Man," she said, reverting to her childhood nickname for him.

He shook his head, denying his mother the opportunity to appease her sudden guilt. He had feelings of his own with which to grapple. "I'm done. This is it for me. I will never keep another secret for anyone, so you have tonight to tell the family about Lincoln or I will," he said before turning and striding away.

His booted feet ate up the stairs as he descended them. Reaching the first floor, he moved quickly to the closet and yanked his coat from the wooden hanger, causing it to tumble to the floor.

"You good, bro?"

Cole glanced at Gabe coming down the last few stairs to also reach for his coat. He'd also picked up the hanger Cole had sent to the floor in his haste.

"Yeah," he lied. "You?" Discovering their father had once cheated on their mother had to have affected his brother, too.

"No," Gabe admitted, opening the door and entering the vestibule. "Affairs. You keeping one hell of a secret from me. A half-brother we have never met. No, I am not good."

Cole was glad to see Harvey already parked on the street and awaiting them.

"I called him," Gabe said, answering the unspoken question.

Bzzzzzz. Bzzzzzz. Bzzzzzz.

"Great," Cole said as he pulled his cell phone from the inner pocket of his coat.

For a moment, he wished it were Jillian.

He shook his head at his mother's number. "Nope," he said, sending the call to voice mail before dropping the phone back into his coat pocket as he bent his body to enter the back seat of the SUV.

He shivered from the cold and was thankful when Harvey slammed the door closed and rushed around the vehicle to do the same for Gabe.

"We never did get him to admit he had us all investigated," Cole said just as Gabe's phone rang. "Unless it was Mom."

"Actually, my bet is on her after the stunts she pulled with Monica and Jillian," Gabe said, pulling his phone from his pocket. "I'm glad to be out of there. I'm going home. Eat some dinner. Love on my woman and go to bed, because reality sucks right now."

Cole shook his head with a snarky laugh when Gabe showed him their mother was calling him now.

"Bonjour," Gabe said in greeting as he checked the time on his gold watch.

Cole ignored his brother's conversation in French as he looked out the window. He was stunned by the knowledge that his mother had been aware of his father's infidelity. Discovering that she'd known, forgiven his father, and seemed to still forge a loving relationship, was forcing him to rethink a lot of things—and to wonder even more.

What private circumstances could have led to his mother forgiving him?

That, he didn't know. But he was now well aware that the role of the blind hapless victim within which he'd placed his mother had been wrong.

How long had she known?

Cole pinched the bridge of his nose, ready to get home to nurse a bottle of rare Scotch from his well-stocked bar.

"Vous ne pouvez pas vous attendre à ce que nous prétendions que c'est tout normal et juste manger le dîner avec tout le monde qui est désemparé de ce qui se passe?" Gabriel said.

Cole gave him a glance, agreeing with what he'd said. *You can't expect us to pretend it's all normal and just eat dinner with everyone who is clueless to what's going on?*

He was sure his brothers had known of their arrival

and were wondering about their speedy departure. He regretted not speaking to them and taking a moment to hug his niece. He had just felt an urgency to get out of there.

"Je suis d'accord avec Cole. Dis-leur. Ou nous le ferons. Plus de secrets!" Gabe's hand urgently slashed the air. *I agree with Cole. Tell them. Or we will. No more secrets.*

Cole pulled his phone from his pocket and swiped until he was looking down at a photo of Jillian the night of the relaunch of Cress, INC.'s website. Her smile was infectious, and that dress was burned into his memory.

What is she doing?

Hopefully, not Warren.

His grip tightened on the phone.

"Je vais lui demander," Gabe said, looking briefly in his direction.

"Ask me what?" Cole said as he tucked his cell phone away.

He listened as Gabe explained that their parents wanted to read the report and reach out to Lincoln for a DNA test to confirm paternity before telling their other brothers.

"No. No more secrets," Cole said with a firm shake of his head. "We can all wait for the results together. We know. They should know. They *will* know, if it's left to me."

Gabe finished the conversation with his mother and ended the call. "Family meeting tomorrow night at the townhouse at eight," he said.

Cole nodded as Harvey brought the SUV to a stop in front of his condo and he let himself out.

Long after he entered his condo and lit the fireplace before pouring himself a stiff drink, he had a reckoning that would not be denied. He was plagued by thoughts of Jillian, their relationship, and where it had all gone wrong—and just what role his knowledge of his father's infidelity may have subconsciously played in that.

Jillian crossed her arms at her chest as she walked around the studio apartment in the Meatpacking District of Manhattan. It didn't compare with the moderate-size loft apartment she'd given up for her move to California, but it was more budget-friendly—and that was key. Most important, it was freedom from her parents' home where late-night giggles and a squeaky bed frame made her life a living hell.

Knock-knock-knock.

She turned from her view of the building across the street to stride the short distance to the door. She gave the movers a thankful smile for working during such frigid weather to transport her furniture from her storage unit after a request of just an hour ago. "Lunch is on me," she said to the two men, waving her hand at a large pot of chili and cheesy cornbread on the stove.

"Now that sounds like a plan," the muscled owner said.

Jillian jammed the door open with a wood wedge and moved out of their way.

Getting the key to the apartment that morning

from the property manager had been the good news she needed. She sat on the window seat and pulled her knees to her chest as she looked out at the gentrified neighborhood that had shifted from its factory roots. Now it's where she called home.

At the sight of a tall man on a motorcycle parking in front of the building, she straightened and pressed her hands to the window.

Cole.

She felt foolish when the man pulled off his helmet, revealing he was not Cole at all.

Of course.

He didn't know where she lived and didn't seem to care to find out.

It was over.

She'd chanced it and lost. And it hurt. If Cole had dropped to his knees, asked her to marry him, she would have. Without question.

"And then I would have *three* ex-husbands," she muttered, resting her chin atop one of her knees as she settled back on the window seat.

"You said something, Miss Rossi?" one of the movers asked.

She glanced at the young man with skin as dark as midnight. He really was attractive. "Ms.," she corrected with the hint of a smile. "I have two ex-husbands making me anything but a Miss."

"Their loss," he said with an appreciative eye.

He was young and fit with a beautiful smile. Just the type to have a wonderful afternoon of fun with—if Cole didn't already occupy her thoughts, keeping her from letting any other man occupy her bed.

No matter how much she missed a man—one particular man—in her bed.

She gave him a shake of her head to gently curtail any attempt at his garnering her attention. He gave her a regretful look and another flirtatious smile before leaving the apartment.

She was thankful when the movers were done in the apartment, having finished setting her belongings where she liked and enjoying the chili she'd prepared. The space was so small that she'd felt cramped with the two men in it. As soon as she closed the door behind them, she turned to lean against it in relief as she looked around.

This was her new life.

A small apartment. Single. Heartbroken.

And lonesome.

Again.

She kicked off her fuzzy slippers and tucked her bare feet beneath her bottom as she sat on her leather sofa. She scrolled through photos of her and Cole. Smiling at some things. Laughing at others. Getting heated at a few that were X-rated.

She was so tempted to call him. Question him. Push back against his misconceptions about her.

Jillian looked at a photo she'd sneaked of him as he'd stepped out of the shower.

Plead with him.

Her eyes dipped down to his package. Sex was the only thing they could do right.

But she wanted more.

"I need more," she said, dropping the phone and once again—for what seemed the millionth time—wrestling the urge to call him.

Love was in the mix and there was no more going back to casual sex when her heart was on the line.

She stood and walked over to her kitchenette to pour herself a glass of red wine. "*He* was wrong. *He* ended things. *He* should call me," she said before taking a deep sip.

He broke my heart.

She turned and leaned her buttocks against the counter.

He accused me of wanting more with Warren.

She took another sip.

And said I was being cruel to Warren.

Another sip.

And cut me loose as if I would ever hurt him.

And another.

Her emotions swelled as she remembered the look on Cole's face when he'd agreed that she should leave. Betrayals were difficult—whether done by someone else or self-inflicted when ignoring a resolve not putting one's heart on the line again.

Jillian felt foolish for giving her power away. She tipped her head back to empty the glass before looking into its emptiness and feeling a kinship. Her tears replaced the wine. They fell with far too much ease.

And that, too, felt like a betrayal.

With a cry that was as jagged as the cuts to her heart, she gripped the glass before throwing it against the wall to shatter.

Eleven

All five Cress brothers were sitting in the den of the family townhouse. There was no staff. The kitchen, living room and dining room were empty. Silence ruled the room.

Phillip Junior paced in front of the elaborate fireplace, lit to help heat the room.

Sean chuckled at videos on his cell phone as he lounged near the closed patio doors.

Gabe refilled his brandy snifter from atop the wide glass-and-brass bar beneath the seventy-inch television on the wall.

Lucas lounged in one of the light gray suede chairs as he texted away on his phone.

Cole eyed them from where he leaned against the entryway between the den and dining room.

"Does anyone know what this meeting is about?" Phillip Junior asked.

Cole and Gabe shared a look.

Lucas frowned, looking up just as they did. "Care to share?" he asked, his voice as deep as his brothers' and father's.

That drew the curious stares of the other Cress brothers.

"Maybe they're ready to announce the new CEO," Phillip Junior said, sounding hopeful.

Sean leaned forward to set his elbows atop his knees as he looked from Cole to Gabe. "Did you get it?" he asked Gabe, speaking everyone's awareness that the middle child—the good one—was favored for the position.

"Remember, I made it clear I don't want it," Gabe said before glancing at his watch. "My restaurant and the position I have at the company is enough on my plate."

All eyes landed on Cole.

"Really?" he asked in disbelief. "Me? Don't be foolish."

"Right." Phillip Junior looked reassured by the reminder that Phillip Senior and Cole had a turbulent relationship.

Cole frowned. Deeply. "I would point out the disgust I feel for you enjoying that I don't have the greatest relationship with our father, but you have enough to tackle tonight, big brother," he said, glancing at his watch.

"What the hell does that mean?" Phillip Junior exclaimed.

"Cole," Gabe intervened.

Footsteps echoed throughout the house. The men all shifted their gaze as their mother and father crossed the kitchen and stepped into the stylish den. Nicolette gave them each a soft smile, looking pretty and regal in the fuchsia pantsuit she wore with her hair pulled back into a low ponytail. In his three-piece suit, Phillip Senior's face seemed more severe as he placed an arm around his wife's shoulders and pressed a kiss to the top of her head.

"We have some news to share…" their father began, his British accent echoing.

If it were at all possible for a room to become more silent, then that best described the environment. Cole looked down at the tip of polished handmade boots as he awaited the reaction of his brothers.

"It has been brought to our attention that when I was eighteen, I unknowingly fathered a child," Phillip Senior said, sticking to his no-nonsense persona. "A son."

And, like the Fourth of July, the questions and exclamations fired off like fireworks in rapid succession.

"What!" Lucas said, his eyes wide and confused.

"Are you serious?" Sean asked.

Phillip Junior threw his hands up in the air. "What does this mean for Cress, INC.?"

"Ça suffit!" Nicolette exclaimed.

Cole, like Gabe, remained silent. He looked on as his brothers sat, expressions full of shock, as their mother pressed a hand to their father's chest when he clutched her closer to him.

Phillip Senior pressed another kiss to his wife's brow

before releasing her to move into the center of the room and boldly eyeing each of his sons. "Yesterday, a preliminary DNA was done and the results came in today," he said. "So far, it has confirmed he is, indeed, my son. Your family. And once the results of the court-approved DNA results return in the next few days, he will also be an heir."

This time his words brought silence. It was stiff. And awkward. And uneasy.

Even Cole took a beat to accept his father's declaration. He had never assumed his father would turn over a key to the kingdom with such ease for a man he'd never known.

"Just like that?" Phillip Junior asked, his jaw stiffening.

"Absolutely, son," Phillip Senior said with a stern expression as he looked at him. "Maybe more so than *any* of you."

Cole's eyes pierced his profile.

"What does that mean?" Gabe asked, breaking his silence.

Phillip Senior shifted his stance. "You have all benefitted from the legacy your mother and I created. It has served each of you well. He received nothing from me and did it all on his own," he said, with a rare reveal of emotion.

That surprised Cole. And rattled him a bit.

Displays of affection from their father were only doled out to their mother once the brothers had become young men. With Phillip Senior, there had been nothing but sternness and a steadfast desire to raise men.

"I never turned my back on any of my sons, and I won't do it now," Phillip Senior said before looking directly at Cole. "*None* of you."

"And is this stranger eligible to be the new CEO of Cress, INC.?" Phillip Junior asked, sounding accusatory.

Phillip Senior turned his head to look at him. "'Stranger'?" he said, his voice filling with coldness. "He is your brother. The same as all the rest."

"I disagree with that," Phillip Junior said.

Steps against the hardwood floor suddenly echoed.

Everyone in the den turned their head just as a man stepped into the room. He was tall, with a shortbread complexion like their own, and a similar face to a twenty-years-younger Phillip Senior.

Cole recognized him from Bobbie's report before their father beckoned the man further into the room with a wave of his hand and introduced him.

"Phillip Junior, Sean, Gabriel, Coleman and Lucas… This is Lincoln Cress. Your brother."

Jillian pushed up her rarely used spectacles as she gave the sprawling double-height kitchen one last perusal before sliding her cutlery set into her satchel. She was done with her chef duties for the day and ready to get to her tiny apartment for a hot foot soak and then a bubble bath. "ASAP," she said.

Bzzzzzz. Bzzzzzz. Bzzzzzz.

She paused to remove her cell phone from the pocket of her chef's coat. "Hey, Ma," she said, tucking the phone between her shoulder and ear as she finished buttoning her overcoat before leaving the empty house via the mudroom.

She rushed to her beloved Mazda Miata as the brutal northeast winter wind whipped around. She was thankful there was no snow to tackle on her lengthy commute to Manhattan.

"I'm at the rehab facility with your grandma," Nora said. "I went to make the monthly payment at the billing office. The account balance had been paid in full. Did you do it?"

Jillian was too busy wishing she had cranked the car and warmed it up before getting into it to really pay attention to her mother's words. "Did I do what, Ma?" she asked as she leaned over to make sure the heat was coming on.

"Did you pay your grandmother's bill in full at the rehab facility?" Nora asked.

Jillian sat straight. "Definitely not," she said, shifting her eyes to her reflection in the rearview mirror.

"Maybe it's an error," Nora said, sounding concerned.

"Did you ask them who paid it?" Jillian asked as she reversed Cherry across the paved courtyard and accelerated forward down the long, winding driveway leading to the main road.

"They said an unidentified benefactor who wished to remain anonymous."

Cole.

"It was Cole," Ionie said in the background, echoing Jillian's thought.

Could he?

With ease. The sum would be of little consequence to him.

Would he?

That was the question.

Did he?

She shook her head. Why would he do such a thing when they weren't even speaking?

"*If* it was Cole, then we will have to pay it back," Jillian insisted.

"Of course," Norah agreed. "But still, *if* it was him, it was a very generous offering. So very gallant."

"Gallant?" Jillian drawled.

"Yes, it seems like the appropriate time to use such a word," Norah said.

She chuckled with her mother.

"Call him. Ask him. And if it was him—*thank* him, Jillie," Ionie said, her speech still a little hesitant.

Jillian pulled to a stop at a red light. She felt nervous at the thought of reaching out to Cole. It was a mix of excitement at hearing his deep voice and fear that he wouldn't answer. "I'll call him," she said. "Let me get back to you, Ma."

She ended the call and dropped the phone onto the passenger seat. As she continued her ride home in silence, she thought of every possible scenario of just what might happen when she called him. None of it ended well.

But why would he pay the bill—if he paid the bill.

There was only one way to know.

And I have to know.

She had not yet struck up the courage to call him by

the time she reached home and gave in to her desires for a foot soak. As she drew a hot bubble bath in her claw-foot tub, her eyes kept going to her phone sitting on the edge of the sink. She *wanted* to talk to Cole.

And more.

Maybe we should give each other some space.

The last words he'd spoken had been enough to keep her from reaching out. She assumed he would decide the space between them was no longer needed. She hoped he would fight for her the same way she had laid her heart out on the line and fought for him. Wooed him. Chased him. Proved she loved him.

It hurt that he hadn't reciprocated.

She eyed the phone again. Curiosity was killing her like the cat. She raised her hand from the water and dried it on the towel hanging over the side before reaching for her phone. Her heart beat so rapidly as she pulled up his contact and dialed his number. She eased her knees up to her chest as the phone started to ring. When it went to voice mail, all of her fears rose along with tears of regret and sadness.

She set the phone back on the sink and rested the side of her face atop her knees. "To hell with love," she muttered, lifting a handful of bubbles to her mouth to blow them up into the air.

Bzzzzzz. Bzzzzzz. Bzzzzzz.

Her head shot up and she looked over at the screen of her phone. A picture of Cole was on it. She felt excited, like a middle school girl receiving a call from her first crush. And just as nervous.

She reached for the phone and answered his call.

"Hello?" she said, wincing when it came out like the strangled cry of a rooster with a hand around its neck.

"Jillian?" he said.

He sounded uncertain even though she was sure her name had displayed on his Caller ID.

Unless he erased your contact.

She raised her wet hand to squeeze the space between her eyebrows. "Yes, it's Jillian. How are you, Cole?" she asked, keeping her tone measured.

"I'm good. You?"

Jillian closed her eyes. They sound so formulaic. So awkward. Stilted. So much like strangers than former lovers.

"Am I bothering you? Are you busy? With work… or someone?" she asked, unable to deny the desire to know if he had completely moved on from her.

The line went silent.

With every passing moment, her pulse increased, and her stomach was a pit of growing nerves. "I understand if it's none of my business—"

"I'm not seeing anyone," he said.

Great.

"And you?" he added.

"Do you care if someone else filled the space you asked for?" she asked, instantly regretting letting her hurt lead her.

"Wow. Really, Jillian?" he asked.

She sighed. "Look. I didn't call to argue. My mother says that my grandmother's bill at her rehab facility has been paid in full," she said. "I was wondering if it was you that blessed us in such a way?"

"You never said if you were with someone." Cole avoided her question. "How's your bestie anyway?"

The water had cooled and the bubbles were beginning to fade, so she stood and stepped out of the tub. Water dripped off her curves. "Warren?" she asked as she grabbed a towel to unfold with a snap before she held it in front of her body.

"Who else?" he drawled.

Jillian arched a brow. "Still concerned about him?" she shot back in sarcasm.

He chuckled.

She did not.

"About the bill, do I have you to thank for it?" she asked, directing him back to the question he'd evaded.

Silence.

"Also, my family and I insist on repaying you, if that's the case," Jillian added.

"I'd prefer to discuss it in person," he finally said.

She nodded as she used the side of her hand to wipe away the steam coating the large round mirror over the pedestal sink. In the reflection, her eyes were uneasy. "Uh. Yeah. Sure," she said. "When?"

"The sooner, the better."

She nodded even though he couldn't see her. "I'll be there within the hour," she said.

"See you then," Cole said before ending the call.

Maybe he wants me to sign a promissory note.

Her nerves did not abate as she dried off and dressed in an off-the-shoulder black sweater, with leggings and shiny black, thigh-high boots with heels. She took time with her makeup and hair and then put in her contacts instead of donning her spectacles. A faux sable coat, leather gloves and dangling gold necklaces finished her polished look.

She did not want to look like she felt: single, alone, and hurting from a breakup.

On the drive to Cole's part of town, she tried to prepare herself for seeing him again. He was a man with great magnetism. His looks. Those eyes. That body. Cole Cress was stylish and charming. His vibe was the essence of cool-and-in-control. His eyes could pierce with contempt or charm without question.

When she stepped up to his front door in the hall of the Chelsea apartment building, she truly thought she was prepared to feign nonchalance.

You got this! You. Got. This.

The door opened and Cole stood there looking at her, far too handsome in a navy V-necked sweater and matching cords.

Oh me. Oh my!

She'd been so wrong. So very wrong.

"Come in," he said, stepping back and pulling the door open wider.

She gave him a smile she hoped wasn't awkward as she moved past him. The scent of his cool cologne seemed to surround her and she bit her bottom lip with a wince as she held back a moan of heightened awareness. She jumped when she felt his hands on her shoulders as he helped remove her coat.

Relax, Jillie. Get it together.

But it was hard with his fireplace lit, the lights

dimmed, and a few fat candles glowing around the room. Add him smelling good and looking good...

The heat Jillian felt had nothing to do with the fireplace.

"Hungry? I cooked some dinner," Cole said, hanging her coat in the closet and then moving into the kitchen.

That surprised her, but she just nodded as she walked over to the kitchen. "What smells so good?" she asked, acutely aware of feeling awkward and out of place in Cole's apartment. Somewhere she had once pictured would be her home, as well.

"What's wrong?" Cole asked.

She looked over at him. "Nothing," she lied. "Why?"

"You looked sad just then," he said, pausing in putting on mitts to take something out the oven.

His eyes stayed locked on her and she shifted under his steady gaze.

"I'm good," she said.

Their eyes met and held.

Her heart pounded. She felt breathless. Staring into Cole's eyes, being captivated by him again, was beyond words, thus leaving her speechless.

"Today I met my half-brother Lincoln," Cole said, finally offering a reprieve by turning away from her to pull a heavy-duty sheet pan from the oven.

Her eyes dipped to take in his buttocks.

"Wait! What?" she asked with two hard blinks as his words registered.

"When my father was eighteen and about to go off to college, he fathered a son with a young woman. He left

England not knowing she was pregnant," he explained. "And today, we all met him."

She watched him as he set the pan of roasted Cornish hens and root vegetables with baby potatoes on the counter. "That must have been a shock. Are *you* okay?" she asked, having seen the battle of wills and might between father and son when she'd worked for them.

Cole eyed her again for long unsettling moments before focusing on taking the hens off the pan to rest and trap in the juices. "Yeah," he said, nodding. "There's still so much to question and understand, but Lincoln agreed to come back to New York for a little while to give us all time to figure out what it all means for the family. The brothers."

"How's Phillip Junior?" she asked with an amused expression.

"Traumatized," Cole countered. "I'm sure he skipped dinner and will whine to Raquel all night about no longer being the heir apparent to the Cress throne."

"And Nicolette?"

Cole retrieved a bottle of wine from his wine rack. "Composed," he said.

They shared a knowing look. Nicolette was the queen of composure but beneath the façade she may very well be close to blowing like a geyser.

"I've had some revelations about myself that directly correlate to my relationship with my father," he said, the muscles of his arms straining against the thinness of his sweater as he opened the bottle.

Jillian bit back a gasp that almost escaped her lips and cleared her throat as she followed him into the dining room. "Has that made things better between you?" she asked.

Cole suddenly stopped and turned.

She nearly bumped into him.

He looked down at her. "No," he said. "But it made me realize that I let my issues with him affect us. And I regret that, Jillian."

Everything inside her fluttered. Her heart. Her belly. Her pulse. And the bud nestled between the lips of her intimacy.

"I thought I was here to talk about the medical bills," she whispered, seeking control when her body was ready to relinquish it. "Did you pay them?"

"Yes," he admitted.

"Why, Cole?" she asked, even as she felt light-headed from the intensity of his stare upon her face, the closeness of his body, and the reminder of his regrets about them.

"Because I love you," he said with a simplicity that shook her to her very core.

Jillian closed her lids and pressed a hand to her eyes as she took a step back. It was a reprieve from that pulsing and all too familiar energy between them. "I *can't* let you do that," she insisted as she turned and pressed her back to the wall.

She was overwhelmed by it all.

"You can and you will," he insisted.

Her body shivered, and she knew before she opened her eyes that he now stood in front of her. "Cole—"

"I won't have you focusing more on making money than on enjoying your gift so that you can pay a bill for someone I have come to care for myself," he said, reaching to stroke her cheek with his thumb.

A gasp escaped.

"My father once betrayed my mother and I caught him…" Cole began as his eyes caressed her. "Since I was a teenager, that betrayal that I kept—the secret that I held—shaped everything I thought I knew about love and fidelity. That, plus an ex I discovered only wanted me because I was a Cress, destroyed my trust."

She saw the emotions raging in the gray-blue depths of his eyes. "Oh, Cole," she whispered, reaching to gently hold his wrist and connect with him as he shared with her.

"I never wanted to fall in love and trust anyone with my heart…and then two years ago, I saw you during that interview with my mother," he reminisced. "I fell for you before I even knew it. That's why, when you chose the job over me—"

Jillian rose on her heeled boots and pressed a kiss to his mouth to halt his words in the hope of easing the hurt she now knew she'd caused him. His arms wrapped around her, pressing her body to his as he eased his face against her neck. The first kiss at her pulse brought shivers. The second softened her knees.

She was thankful when he took her up into his strong and able arms. She wrapped hers around his neck. "I have my own confession," she whispered in his ear, feeling him shiver as her breath stroked his lobe. "It's about Warren."

Cole stiffened.

"I spoke to him after what you said and he admitted that he was hoping he and I would get back together," she said. "So, I didn't take the job and told him maybe it was best we saw less of each other because I didn't want his hope to rise."

Cole relaxed. "I thought you were going to say y'all—"

"For the past two years, I have not been with anyone but you, Cole," she admitted.

He lowered her to her feet and then picked her up again, this time with her legs wrapped around his waist so that they were looking at each other. Eye to eye. Mouth to mouth. "Same here," he promised her, his words breezing against her lips.

She believed him.

With a light lick of her lips, she kissed him.

Cole released a moan of hunger as he deepened it with his clever tongue, turning to press her back against the wall. She grabbed his costly sweater into her fists without a care as she kissed him with every bit of passion she had been denied over the weeks. She was starved for it. For him.

Wait!

Jillian jerked her head back to break the kiss. He looked dazed, his mouth covered with her sheer-pink gloss as his eyes filled with confusion. "If you had this wonderful epiphany about us, why did I have to call you, Cole Cress?" she asked, using her thumb to clean his lips.

"I have a surprise for you," he said, carrying her down the hall to his suite.

She released a soft moan at the sight of the lighted candles offering the only illumination in the spacious room other than the moon's shine. Atop the bed were rose petals and the scent of them burst in the air. In the center of the array was another of his notes.

Cole carried her across the room and set her on her feet as he started to undress her. Her eyes stayed locked on the note.

"You did all this since I called. How?" she asked before her sweater went flying over his head.

"Wealth has its benefits," Cole said as he undid her bra.

"This is nice. And *that* is very nice," she said, trembling as he sucked one hard nipple and then the other into his mouth. "But why did I have to call you?"

Cole ignored her as he bent to unzip her boots before removing each along with her sheer socks. He pressed heated kisses to her hips as he slid her leggings and lace thong panties down over her plump bottom and thighs. He turned his head to suck her plump vee with a grunt before giving it a gentle bite.

She cried out and arched her back with a gasp at the pleasure. Naked and shivering before him, Cole looked on as he stepped back from her, his erection pressing against the zipper of his pants as he pulled his sweater over his head, revealing his chiseled chest and abdomen. She closed the gap between them to stroke the flat hairs on his chest before dipping her head to stroke one flat brown nipple with her tongue. "Can I have my note?" she asked as she undid his belt and zipper to work his pants and black boxer briefs around his hard buttocks and even harder inches.

Cole chuckled. "Yes," he said.

Jillian gripped his tool and gently guided him behind her to the side of the bed as she reached for the note with her free hand. Behind it was a red-velvet, heart-shaped ring box. "Oh," she said in surprise.

Cole wrapped an arm around her waist. "All of this I did tonight. But that, I purchased a few days ago," he explained, finally offering the proof of his intentions toward her before her call.

Jillian leaned back against his strength, releasing his erection to clutch her note with both hands as she emotionally choked up.

"I was trying to figure out some grand way to propose and then you called," he further explained. "I went with fate."

Tears welled from the joy of being loved by someone she loved and having him want to share the rest of his life with her. *But* her fears crept up—she couldn't deny that. Opening the note, she smiled at his words, caressing them with her fingertips as she read them aloud. "'I hunger for your love the same as I hunger for your body. Your presence is my comfort zone. Your smile is my light. Making you happy will be my goal for the rest of our lives, my Jillian.'"

Jillian closed her eyes as tears fell. Their affair had begun with a note and it was so romantic of him to propose with one, as well. She wanted nothing more in the world than to believe him. Memories of two failed marriages were her detractors. And she hated that, for Cole and for herself.

Damn.

Cole pressed one knee into the bed to pick up the ring box before turning to sit on the bed in front of her as he opened it.

The ring was exquisite. She loved its unique design and the brilliant sparkle of the large diamond. "Cole," she whispered, seeing the flicker of candlelight in his eyes.

He removed the ring from the box. "Will you—?"

"Wait," she said, reaching to cover the ring and his hand with her own.

He looked up at her, apprehension in his eyes.

Jillian pressed a hand to the side of his face. "Cole, I've been married before—"

"Do you love me?" he asked.

"More than I have ever loved anyone," she said with sincerity.

"Then how can you compare me and what we can build together—trust, love, a family—when you have never had the same love for those other men?" he said. "Who you are now is not who you were then. And I am not them."

"A family?" she asked, pressing her hand to her belly and envisioning it swollen with their child.

Cole covered her hand with his own. "Yes," he stressed.

"Girl or boy?" she asked.

"Girl," they said in unison.

"There're more than enough male Cress family members," Cole said dryly.

Jillian's eyes went back to the ring.

I do love him.

She reread the note.

And he loves me.

She remembered reading something Maya Angelou had said. "'Have enough courage to trust love one more time…'" she quoted the poet.

Cole rose before her. "We both have to leave our past in the past and trust in each other," he said before dropping to his knee. "Let's do it together. Marry me?"

I can't let the hurt caused by other men keep this love from me now.

With a building excitement like nothing she had ever felt, Jillian bit her bottom lip as she raised her left hand, presented it to him, hoping he could see and feel the love she had for him. And as he took her hand in his and slid the weighty jewel onto her finger, she pushed aside her fears, determined to claim her happiness with the man she loved.

Cole stood and kissed her before quickly grabbing her waist and turning her body to lay it down on the bed, sandwiched by the rose petals and his body.

His weight felt familiar. Comfortable. Perfect.

"And what about dinner, my love?" she said, rubbing her leg up and down the length of his as he pressed kisses to her neck.

Cole gave her a wicked smile before moving his body down between her legs as he spread them. "I have everything I want to eat right here," he said before lowering his head to blow a cool stream of air against her intimacy.

Jillian clutched at his head as she arched her back and closed her eyes at the pleasure of his tongue. She rolled her hips and Gabe moaned deep in his throat as his fingers gripped her buttocks. "Yes," she gasped in ecstasy as goose bumps raced across her skin.

She gave in to the pleasure and her love with the hope that they would cherish, honor, and trust one another in a way neither had before with anyone. She was hopeful. Even as she was driven to mindless passion by her love—who seemed hell-bent on pleasing her—she allowed herself to free-fall into the bliss of love and carry Cole—her sexy rebel—right along with her.

Hopefully, for forever and a day.

Epilogue

Three months later

Cole looked over his mother's head as they danced to eye Jillian dancing with her father. There was a smile on her face as she looked up at the tall, broad man with the love a daughter has for her father. His bride looked beautiful in a couture, formfitting, soft tulle gown scattered with delicate beading. The deep V-neckline and detachable overskirt of layers of tulle made her hourglass figure more pronounced. The sheer blush color of the gown was sexy and delicate. She was stunning. Cole smiled and chuckled when Harry surprised her with a dip and Jillian's eyes widened.

I love my wife.

Earlier that afternoon, they had wed at the courthouse. Just the two of them. They had chosen to put their marriage and each other first above all else. They'd wanted the focus on their marriage and not just a lavish wedding ceremony.

The reception was open to all their family and friends, and their wedding planner had magically converted the grand ballroom in the luxury Manhattan hotel to a floral wonderland—just the way Jillian had envisioned it. And that was his goal for the rest of his life. He wanted to make her as happy as she deserved to be.

"Are you happy, son?"

Cole looked down into his mother's blue eyes. In their depths, a genuine concern for him—even if her actions to destroy things between Jillian and him had been her misguided attempt to make his life as easy as possible.

Perhaps to save him from the heartbreak he was sure she'd felt at the discovery of her husband's affair.

"There is no one who could make me any happier," Cole said, giving her the smile he'd used as a young boy to charm her for an extra dessert after dinner.

Nicolette nodded as she blinked away tears. "Okay," she said, her voice soft and resigned to yet another of her sons being with a woman not of her choosing.

"Why did you forgive him?" he asked, his eyes studying his mother's profile.

For the briefest moment, Nicolette's body stiffened and she avoided looking up at him.

"A man's ego is a fragile thing," she said. "And having your wife win a trifecta of James Beard awards, for which both of you were nominated, can weaken a shaky foundation."

Cole saw a flash of pain in her eyes even as she attempted to keep from facing him. He bent his head and pressed a kiss to her temple. "Then he was a childish fool," he said for her ears alone.

Nicolette touched her head to his chest briefly. "I agree," she said, summoning a smile for her son.

The song for the parents' dance ended and everyone applauded before both Cole and Jillian moved toward each other. He wrapped an arm around her waist and pulled her close as he looked into her upturned face. "Ready for our honeymoon?" he asked, her hands stroking his neck as they danced to "All of Me" by John Legend.

"Yes. I can't wait for a week-long vacation in Greece," she said, her eyes sparkling with love and happiness.

"That sounds like you won't miss the food truck," he mused, raising her hand to spin her before pulling her body back to his.

"No offense, but I won't," she said.

Cole chuckled.

Jillian had left behind her coveted position as the private chef of a high-powered movie executive to fulfill her dreams of her own cooking establishment by operating the food truck during the week while Cole was busy with his duties at Cress, INC. On the weekends, they enjoyed working it together, combining their love of food and each other.

"Listen, Jillian…" he said.

"Yes, *husband*," she said.

"I never want you to worry if your light shines brighter than mine that I will resent you or harbor ill feelings toward you. A win for you is a win for us," Cole promised, again shirking ever taking on the bad traits his father possessed.

"A win for you is a win for us. Same difference," she assured him, easing her hands onto his shoulders.

"Always," he vowed before gripping her waist and lifting her to kiss her deeply and with all the passion he could muster without offending their now applauding audience with proof of his arousal.

"And forever," she whispered against his mouth.

* * * * *

#2809 TEXAS TOUGH
Texas Cattleman's Club: Heir Apparent • by Janice Maynard
World-traveling documentary filmmaker Abby Carmichael is only in Royal for a short project, definitely not to fall for hometown rancher Carter Crane. But opposites attract and the sparks between them ignite! Can they look past their differences for something more than temporary?

#2810 ONE WEEK TO CLAIM IT ALL
Sambrano Studios • by Adriana Herrera
The illegitimate daughter of a telenovela mogul, Esmeralda Sambrano is shocked to learn *she's* the successor to his empire, much to the chagrin of her father's protégé, Rodrigo Almanzar. Tension soon turns to passion, but will a common enemy ruin everything?

#2811 FAKE ENGAGEMENT, NASHVILLE STYLE
Dynasties: Beaumont Bay • by Jules Bennett
Tired of being Nashville's most eligible bachelor, Luke Sutherland needs a fake date to the wedding of the year, and his ex lover, Cassandra Taylor, needs a favor. But as they masquerade as a couple, one hot kiss makes things all too real...

#2812 A NINE-MONTH TEMPTATION
Brooklyn Nights • by Joanne Rock
Sable Cordero's dream job as a celebrity stylist is upended after she spends one sexy night with fashion CEO Roman Zayn. When he learns Sable is pregnant, he promises to take care of his child, nothing more. But neither anticipated the attraction still between them...

#2813 WHAT HAPPENS IN MIAMI...
Miami Famous • by Nadine Gonzalez
Actor Alessandro Cardenas isn't just attending Miami's hottest art event for the parties. He's looking to find who forged his grandfather's famous paintings. When he meets gallerist Angeline Louis, he can't resist at least one night...but will that lead to betrayal?

#2814 CORNER OFFICE SECRETS
Men of Maddox Hill • by Shannon McKenna
Chief finance officer Vann Acosta is not one to mix business with pleasure—until he meets stunning cybersecurity expert Sophie Valente. Their chemistry is undeniable, but when she uncovers the truth, will company secrets change everything?

YOU CAN FIND MORE INFORMATION ON UPCOMING HARLEQUIN TITLES, FREE EXCERPTS AND MORE AT HARLEQUIN.COM.

*The illegitimate daughter of a telenovela mogul,
Esmeralda Sambrano-Peña is shocked to learn she's
the successor to his empire, much to the chagrin of her
father's protégé, Rodrigo Almanzar. Tension soon turns
to passion, but will a common enemy ruin everything?*

Read on for a sneak peek at
One Week to Claim It All
by Adriana Herrera.

"I want to kiss you, Esmeralda."

She shook her head at the statement, even as a
frustrated little whine escaped her lips. Her arms were
already circling around his neck. "If we're going to do
this, just do it, Rodrigo."

Without hesitation he crushed his mouth into hers and
the world fell away. This man could be harbor in any
storm, always had been. His tongue stole into her mouth,
and it was like not a single day had passed since they'd
last done this.

She pressed herself to him as he peppered her neck
with fluttering kisses. Somewhere in the back of her mind
she knew this was the height of stupidity, that they were
both being reckless. That if anyone found out about this,
she would probably sink her chances of getting approved

by the board. But it was so hard to think when he was whispering intoxicatingly delicious things in Spanish. *Preciosa, amada… Mia.*

It was madness for him to call her his, and what was worse, she reveled in it. She wanted it so desperately that her skin prickled, her body tightening and loosening in places under his skilled touch.

"I can't get enough of you. I never was able to." He sounded bewildered. Like he couldn't quite figure out how it was that he'd gotten there.

Welcome to the club.

Esmeralda knew they should stop. They were supposed to head to the party soon and she'd for sure have to refresh her makeup now that she'd decided to throw all her boundaries out the window. But instead of stopping, she threw her head back and let him make his way down her neck, his teeth grazing her skin as he tightened one hand on her butt and the other pulled down the strap of her dress.

"Can I kiss you here?" he asked as his breath feathered over her breasts.

"Yes." She was on an express bus to Bad Decision Central and she could not be bothered to stop.

Don't miss what happens next in…
One Week to Claim It All
by Adriana Herrera,
the first book in her new Sambrano Studios series!

Available soon wherever
Harlequin Desire books and ebooks are sold.

Harlequin.com

Get 4 FREE REWARDS!

We'll send you 2 FREE Books <u>plus</u> 2 FREE Mystery Gifts.

Harlequin Desire books transport you to the world of the American elite with juicy plot twists, delicious sensuality and intriguing scandal.

FREE Value Over $20

CHAPTER ONE

There's no place like home.

Huh.

Obviously, Dorothy hadn't gotten out much.

Sydney Collins slowed her car to a stop in front of a
picturesque covered bridge as if the reason for Dorothy's
bewildering need to return to boring sepia-toned Kansas
could be found etched into the red-painted boards.

Sydney could still remember sitting in the living room
and watching *The Wizard of Oz* for the first time when she'd
been seven years old. While her parents and her sister,
Carlin, had been rooting for Dorothy to click those ruby
heels and make it back home, Sydney had jumped to her feet
and yelled, "Are you crazy, Dorothy? Keep your ass in Oz!"

Well, her parents hadn't been too happy with the language—they'd later had words with Uncle Travis about watching his mouth around her—but Carlin, resting in her special recliner, had quietly snickered.

Carlin…

A dusty, too-familiar feeling weaved through Sydney, burrowing deep in her heart. From experience, she knew no amount of meditation, come-to-Jesus talks or Sunday sermons explaining how "God moves in mysterious ways" could dig it out.

Sydney's fingers tightened around the steering wheel until the ridges pressed into her palms. Instead of loosening her grip, she squeezed harder. And harder. The dull throb kept her grounded here, in the present.

God. She hadn't even crossed over the town line, and already the memories were smothering her, seeking to drag her back.

Well, the past wasn't exactly dragging her back. As of yesterday morning, when she'd left Charlotte, North Carolina, to start the twelve-hour drive to the Berkshires, she'd willingly returned to her hometown of Rose Bend, Massachusetts.

The hometown she'd vowed—eight years earlier—to never step foot in again.

Had it been about only her, she still might be settled in her Ballentyne condo.

But it was no longer about only her.

The Road to Rose Bend
by Naima Simone.
Look for it May 2021 from HQN!

HQNBooks.com